BERNARD PALMER

THE WIND
BLOWS WILD

MOODY PRESS

CHICAGO

To my wife, Marjorie,
who has accompanied me without complaint
whenever and wherever I have gone in search
of a story, and who spends uncounted hours
praying, typing and correcting copy. Few
men are blessed with such a helpmate.

AUTHOR'S NOTE

THE WIND BLOWS WILD is a factual novel and the events recorded are true. Most of them actually happened to Albert and Rhoda Tait. All of them could have.

Special appreciation is due the Northern Canada Evangelical Mission, Prince Albert, Saskatchewan, and the missionaries listed below, for making this book possible. The Mission opened its stations to me and made arrangements for me to fly to Island Lake, Manitoba, to complete research on the manuscript.

Reverend and Mrs. Ray Bradford

Reverend and Mrs. Marshall Calverley

Pilot and Mrs. Ed Hickey

Reverend and Mrs. Ray Larson

Reverend and Mrs. Clifford McComb

Mrs. Evelyn Matthews

Mr. and Mrs. Albert Tait

Reverend and Mrs. John Unger

1

Alex LeLiberte had been fighting the wild northern Ontario lake for more than an hour. He angled the scow around the island, past a dangerous finger of rocks that extended two hundred yards into the open lake. The cumbersome fishing boat climbed over one wave, nosed downward and burrowed into the next.

She was a sturdy craft for all her heavy planking and hand-formed lines. Rising doggedly, she spumed icy spray on either side. Alex shuddered as the cold mist caught him full in the face. Briefly he relaxed his hand on the outboard motor. The handle jerked away from him and the boat lurched dangerously as another wave hit her.

"Alex!" his companion shouted. "Watch it or we'll both go for a swim!"

The wind had been coming up steadily since sundown the

5

night before. It snarled through the jack pine and poplar and pounded long, deep-troughed breakers savagely against the island.

Earlier in the morning the ugly gray clouds had pressed down against the trees, spitting rain into the gathering gale. With the coming of daylight the rain had stopped, but the cold remained. It drove through Alex's thin jacket and stiffened his rubber overalls.

Alex hunched against the wet and cold and tried to think of something else. He and Joseph had been on the rough water since dawn, lifting nets and filling boxes with whitefish and jacks and pickerel. He longed to be inside again—to stand by a crackling wood fire and feel the pain soak out of his bones, to sit down to a meal of moose stew and bannock or macaroni. The day was miserable and bone-chilling, the sort that made fishermen long for jobs ashore.

As they neared the net he turned the controls to Joseph and braced himself against the violent pitching of the boat. With deft, sure movements he leaned over, jerked the net marker from the water and grasped the line.

The cold soaked through the cotton gloves and bit into his cramped fingers. A sudden, convulsive chill seized him. Grimly he shivered and began to raise the net. Icy water ran off the nylon strands and trickled down the heavy rubber of his overalls to make the floor dangerously slick.

But Alex scarcely noticed. The sooner they got the fish out of the net the sooner they would get ashore where they could get warm again. Working so rapidly he grew careless and dropped his hook. It went skittering across the floor. For an instant caution left him and he turned quickly and stooped. At the same time the boat lurched and Alex was hurled against the side, almost toppling into the frigid lake.

Joseph chuckled, revealing his yellow, scraggly teeth.

"The lake is for fish, Alex!"

A quick grin flashed across the young Soulteaux Indian's dark face. "Is that so?" he retorted.

6

Alex and his companion went back to work again. The catch in the net was good, but not the prized whitefish and pickerel. They were getting jacks, and the price for them was as miserable as the weather.

Jackfish were too bony, the buyer said, and the flavor didn't quite suit the delicate taste of the white man in the States, even under the elegant name of northern pike.

Briefly Alex's temper flared. The white man ought to have to eat from a bare cupboard like he and Rose had back at Round Lake. He ought to find out what it was like to have the Hudson Bay store cut his credit off. If his belly got empty enough, or he heard the pitiful crying of his baby for food as Alex had, he'd soon find that jacks were good enough for anybody.

Alex glanced back at his companion. Joseph was very much as he had been when he took his first fishing job. His face was smooth and lean and the fire of youth flamed in his dark eyes. Alex knew that fire well. It led a boy to drinking and gambling and stealing and the wrong kind of girls. Not so many years before it had flamed in his own eyes, driving him relentlessly into a path he couldn't resist.

And he hadn't been able to do anything about it himself. Not until the missionary told him about God.

He had planned to talk with Joseph about those things in the long evenings when they sat alone in the cabin. He even put his Bible on a shelf near his chair, where he could get it easily. But it had lain there for days, untouched and gathering dust.

There had been a time when he would have made excuse to talk to Joseph, when he would have spent their first night together telling what Jesus had done for him. That was back when his heart burned for his people, when there was nothing in the world so important as telling someone else about the changes Jesus Christ could make in their lives. That was in the days when he had been sure he would spend the rest of his life bringing Christ to his people.

Now he was finished with that. And for good reason.

A man couldn't let his wife and baby go hungry. And unless he trapped or fished, he couldn't get credit at the store. No matter how badly he wanted to serve the Lord he couldn't spend all his time interpreting for the missionary or talking to people about God.

Rose hadn't said anything when he quit work to spend his time helping the missionary. She had come home from the hospital with their new baby, excited over his chance to help the missionary.

"I think it's good, Alex." She eyed him shyly. "I served God too while I was in the hospital."

"They think maybe there'll be money for us. Somebody from the States sends it."

"Yes?" she echoed.

"We will help win the people at Round Lake for Christ."

She nodded. "It is good to work for God, Alex."

It had been good as long as the money came in. But when it began to dwindle as the people in the States got careless about sending it, it was not so good.

At first Alex managed to ignore what was happening. After all, they had credit enough at the Bay to buy flour for bannock and macaroni, and a little tea. Finally, however, the manager began to ask when they could pay their bill.

"We've been cut off," Rose warned him on returning from the store. "We won't get credit anymore until we pay on the bill."

"Some money will come in soon. I'll talk to him. I'll get him to wait."

"He won't wait." Fear glittered in Rose's dark eyes. "He says we have to pay on the bill." She glanced at the thin, pinched face of the baby in the *takinakan* propped beside her against the wall. He started to whimper and she began to rock the cradleboard gently to quiet him. "The baby's very hungry. He cries all the time."

Alex left the house uneasily. The missionary said God

would take care of them. He said God would give them food to stop the crying of the baby and wipe the hurt from Rose's tender heart.

But He hadn't. Now they were out of both money and food. It was enough to drive a man back to fishing.

He went to the bay first to talk to the manager about more credit.

"Money will come in on the next mail, maybe," he explained.

The manager's expression did not change. "I'm sorry, Alex, but you know company policy. When the bill gets so big there is no more credit." He shrugged his shoulders. "There's nothing I can do."

An hour later Alex appeared at the missionary's door. Cooper asked him in and, as is the custom among the northern Indians, they visited endlessly before getting to the purpose of the visit. At last Alex got to his feet. Cooper followed him to the door.

"You look sad," he said gently.

He did not reply.

"Are you having trouble, Alex?"

The Indian nodded almost imperceptibly and went back to a chair near the stove. It was not easy to speak of such things to one like the missionary. He knew the gaunt, angular Cooper would be displeased. He might even be angry. And it was not in Alex's nature to deliberately incur the wrath of one he called friend.

For a long while he waited, struggling within himself. Silence did not seem to bother the towering missionary as it did some white men. Crossing his legs he waited patiently until the youthful Soulteaux framed his tortured thoughts into words. Eventually Alex was ready to speak.

"We don't have anything in our cupboard to eat," he explained, hands working nervously. "No milk for the baby even."

"Have you asked God for food?" Cooper asked.

There was no harshness in his voice, Alex noted gratefully. Only genuine concern. This missionary was not like other

9

white men he had known. He *cared* that there was no food for the baby.

"Have you asked God for food?" Cooper repeated.

"I asked Him." The corners of the young Soulteaux's mouth twitched. "I asked Him, but He didn't hear. It doesn't matter to Him that I have to borrow or beg to eat. Other people who don't serve God have milk for their babies. Even when I was a lost sinner my belly was full."

He leaned forward, brown eyes searching for answers in the other man's face.

The missionary was as careful in his reply as Alex had been in forming his complaint. He reminded him of God's loving kindness—that God did know and care, that He would provide for Rose and little Ernest.

"We will pray for God's help."

When he finally was ready to leave Cooper excused himself and came back with a small sack of flour and some macaroni.

"We don't have much," he explained. "Our support hasn't been coming in regularly either, but this may help a little."

Alex took it gratefully.

God would take care of him and his family now, he acknowledged thankfully. It said so in the Bible and he and Cooper prayed about it. Already He had seen that they got enough to eat for a couple of days. Alex felt better as he trudged across the settlement to the little cabin he had built himself.

Not so with Rose. Her shrill voice crescendoed in anger.

"Cooper says we get food from God!" she exclaimed, bitterness twisting her full young mouth. "All I know is that our baby is hungry and we are hungry and there is nothing to eat."

"There is the grub Cooper gave us," he protested feebly.

She snorted and thumped the sack with her hand.

"Enough for one day maybe," she exploded, "or two if we do not eat much. What do we do then, Alex? Go back and ask him for more when there is hardly enough for his own family?" Her expression softened. "Don't you see, Alex? You have to go to work!"

10

When that tone came into her voice there was no arguing with it. Besides, his own discouragement came surging back. What Cooper said about God taking care of them might be true enough, but Alex was not even sure of that. If God was going to help, why didn't He help now? Why would He let little Ernest cry because there was nothing for him to eat? Why would He let Rose grow cross and disagreeable with worry?

"But there is no work here."

That was when they decided she would take the baby to Sachigo to stay with her parents while he went to Red Lake to find a job fishing.

Not that Alex liked living alone. It was not good for a man to be without his family. Nor was it easy for Rose to live with her parents, even for a short time.

He knew what her people would be saying. Her father was the most influential man in the isolated little village. Influential and proud. He had raged when she told him of her decision to follow Christ. Now he would have new fuel for his assault against her.

"This happens because God is mad at you and Alex, Rose," he would be saying. "He will curse you or something because you leave your church."

Alex knew his beautiful young wife well enough to know she would never complain in her infrequent letters. That was not her way. Nor would she lift her voice against the railing of her father. But the hurt would be there, deep and gnawing. The hurt and the loneliness.

Alex removed another fish from the net, pulling the tough nylon thread from about its middle with the steel hook, and paused momentarily.

He missed Rose's shy smile and the soft caress of her eyes as she looked at him. She was her mother's daughter when she was excited or angry. On those occasions her eyes flashed and her voice grew barbed and imperious. Alex had learned to recognize the mood and to get out of the house until her anger

11

spent itself. Most of the time however she was gentle and tender, the sort of wife a man dreamed about as the mother of his children. That was what he remembered now that they were apart.

That and the baby. He missed the tiny form of the little one who looked so much like himself it startled him. He even missed the crying that had increased so much in the last weeks before he left Round Lake to go fishing.

"Hurry, Alex!" Joseph chided, breaking into his thoughts. "I'm cold!"

Mechanically he went back to work.

At last they removed the final fish from the net. Joseph started the motor and opened the throttle carefully. The fish-ladened scow came about and began to plow through the waves. As they neared the shore Alex saw a tall, uniformed figure standing alone on the dock.

The Royal Canadian Mounted Police! Why would a mountie have come all the way out from the village? His blood chilled.

"What did you do the last time you were in town, Joseph?" he asked uneasily. "Is he after you?"

"Me? Why do you think he comes after me? I do nothing to bring him here." He squinted nervously at the officer.

Several minutes later they nosed into the dock.

"*Waaci*,"* the officer said in Indian. He took their line and snubbed the boat to the weathered post nearest them.

Joseph clambered out and fastened the stern line.

"Which of you is Alex LeLiberte?"

Alex's expression did not betray the turmoil that seized him. He was trembling inside when he climbed out of the boat and looked up into the officer's steel-blue eyes.

"I have a message for you."

The young Soulteaux's hands shook as he opened the envelope and read it. A wave of nausea swept over him.

"I am sorry, Alex," the mountie said. "Is there anything I can do?"

*Hello.

12

He shook his head. There was nothing anybody could do. Not when his only son was dead!

Alex turned abruptly and stumbled off the dock, suddenly unmindful of the wind and cold. A wave slid up the rocky beach, covering his rubbers and soaking his moccasins, but he scarcely noticed. For the moment he was numb and unfeeling.

Ernest was dead.

That was all he knew—all that mattered. His only son who looked so much like him, even from the day Rose brought him back to Round Lake from the hospital where he was born.

Alex had planned so much for his son. So much that was different than his own miserable childhood.

He stared across the wind-lashed lake that somehow reminded him of his own tortured life as a boy.

It was strange he would think of such things now. He hadn't remembered them for years.

Things would probably have been different for him if his mother hadn't died. She gave her life bringing him into the world and ever since he could remember he had been knocked around from one home to another. Nobody really wanted him. He was just one more mouth to feed. But they had to take him in. It was the way of their people.

Even thinking about what it was like when he was young brought hurt to him.

2

When Alex LeLiberte was seven years old, he marched purposefully up the steps of McDonald's Trading Post. Old McDonald would storm at him. He always did. But this time he wouldn't chase him out. He was at the free trader's store on business. His bony fist clutched a carefully penciled list from his older brother, Pete.

Pete had a job in the mine and got paid every week. He wasn't dependent upon the uncertain fortunes of trapping or fishing. McDonald welcomed the credit business of the miners. He wouldn't risk making Pete angry.

Alex stopped before the door, savoring the moment expectantly. This was one he was going to enjoy.

Bracing his feet he heaved on the big door with all the strength in his puny arms. It inched open and he pushed inside. Old McDonald was standing behind the counter, glowering at him over his spectacles.

"Alex," the trader warned. "I told you not to come in here."
Triumphantly the boy held up a list.

"Pete wants you to sell me these. He said for you to put them on his bill. When he gets his check next week he come in and pay you."

The storekeeper squinted at the order. It was a long one.

"Well!" A smile warmed his face.

Still smiling he moved toward the back of the building. Alex sidled closer to the counter, but not without McDonald's knowledge.

"Stay right where ye are, lad," the trader muttered darkly, "an' keep your thievin' fingers in your pockets or I'll tell your brother on ye an' he'll skin ye alive."

"I ain't took nothin'." There was an injured tone in Alex's voice, as though he had never been guilty of appropriating items that didn't belong to him.

"No, an' ye ain't goin' to. Not iffen I can help it."

McDonald glared at him until he scuffed reluctantly to the middle of the wide board floor a safe distance from the temptingly ladened tables and shelves. Even then the graying, portly old trader was not satisfied. He stared at Alex until he was content there was nothing within reach. Only then did he set to work. He noted Pete LeLiberte's list and looked up at Alex. When he was sure the boy had not moved he searched frantically for the item in his stock, moving so rapidly sweat soon stood out on his face and beaded his bald head.

The Indian lad grinned inwardly. He had old McDonald going this time. That was sure. He eyed him and waited for the chance he hoped would come.

At last McDonald found the final item, painstakingly added up the bill, and thrust the sack into the boy's outstretched arms.

"Now see ye don't fool around on the way home. Hear me?"

Alex's face was expressionless, but his heart hammered fiercely and his hands were moist with sweat. When old McDonald shoved the sack at him it pressed hard against the heavy hunting knife under his shirt. The storekeeper knew! He had to! Alex had been a fool to think he could get away with anything so big as a hunting knife.

His gaze met McDonald's, but the old man's smile came back.

"Tell Pete 'tis a pleasure to serve 'im. Tell 'im to send a list an' I'll put it up for him anytime, eh?"

Alex mumbled under his breath and began to shuffle toward the door. It wasn't his conscience that bothered him. It was McDonald. The old storekeeper was too wary to be fooled very often.

Alex fumbled with the latch. It didn't open immediately and panic seized him. What if McDonald had locked him in?

Then the door opened and he hurried out, almost dropping the sack of grub in his haste. The store owner stared after him uneasily.

"Ye didn't happen to see that LeLiberte kid over at the counter, did ye, Otto?" he asked another customer who was still waiting.

"Not more'n a minute."

McDonald groaned.

"That's all the time he needs. The fact is, it's more'n he needs. If he could carry it, he could walk off with half the store in a minute and you'd never see him snitch a thing!"

As he spoke he waddled over to the counter nearest the place where Alex stood and began to check the stock that was out in the open. He wasn't long in discovering what was missing.

"My best hunting knife!" he exploded. "Six dollars and forty cents wholesale!"

Ponderously he ran to the front door and out on the porch, puffing with exertion. Alex was scurrying along the path, but was still in sight.

"LeLiberte!" McDonald thundered, menacingly shaking his fist in the air. "Come back here! Come back here!"

Alex heard him. He almost died when the angry storekeeper

16

shouted his name. But he did not stop. Instead his moccasined feet flew even faster over the rough path.

McDonald remained on the porch, shouting at him until he was out of sight. Only then did he turn and come back inside, anger purpling his heavy jowls.

"That thievin' young rascal we'll see behind bars one day," he muttered.

"How right ye are, Alister," Otto Magnuson retorted. "He's one Soulteaux we'll both live to see hanged."

Once he was out of sight of the storekeeper Alex stopped, drawing in his breath in long, tearing gasps. If McDonald had been going to follow him he'd be coming by this time. That meant he had lost his chance to prove that Alex had the knife. If he was accused all he'd have to do would be to deny it, assuming he could find a good enough place to hide it. And he didn't doubt his own ability to do that.

A heady exhilaration swept over him. There wasn't any doubt about it. He was getting pretty slick.

Setting the sack of grub on the ground, he took the knife from beneath his shirt and examined it carefully. It had a good feel to it and the blade gleamed so brightly he could see his impish young reflection in its side. For an instant he examined himself, enjoying what he saw. His smile widened as he ran his finger lightly over the razor edge.

There wasn't a better knife in all of Sachigo Mine than this one. A guy could skin a moose with it, if he killed one. For the moment he wished himself older so he could kill a moose and skin it with his fine new knife.

He had thought a lot about saving enough money to get one for himself, but he had never supposed he would make it. Now he had one and it hadn't cost him anything. The only trouble was he couldn't show it to anyone. At least not for a long time.

He'd have to hide the knife before he took the grub into the house. Old McDonald was right about one thing. Pete would half knock his head off if he found out about it. Thoughtfully,

17

Alex picked up the sack and continued in the direction of Pete's cabin. He'd hide the knife in a secret place under the porch and only take it out to look at it when he was sure his older brother was gone.

If Alister McDonald made good his threat and told Pete about the knife, Alex would just have to lie and hope he could make his brother believe him. He felt the hunting knife against the flat of his stomach. If Pete found out about it he'd get a beating, but it was worth the risk. Excitement tingled up Alex's spine as he reached home and carefully hid the knife away.

* * *

Alex hated living with his oldest brother, but that didn't seem to matter to anybody. Pete and his wife took him in, reluctantly, but they took him, so that was where he lived most of the time. Still, he was an extra in their house and they didn't let him forget it. When he was five years old Pete's wife, Ella, had work for him to do.

"You help with the dishes and the sweeping, Alex," she ordered. "You bring in wood and take care of the kids when I want you to."

Anger flecked his defiant brown eyes. He didn't say anything. If he did he was answered with a kick or a clout on the head that made his ears ring. So he kept silent, his resentment smouldering.

Taking care of Pete and Ella's kids wasn't shame enough. He was also pressed into looking after the children of the women who lived nearby.

"I want Alex to watch my baby," a mother would say to Pete or his wife. "I'm going fishing today."

The answer was always the same. "Bring him over. Alex will watch him."

And when she came to get the baby once her work was done, she would bring some fish or blueberries or a piece of dried moose meat for the grub box. That was all Ella cared about.

18

It didn't matter to her that she brought ridicule and shame to her husband's youngest brother.

Among the Soulteaux, boys didn't take care of younger children or wash dishes. Most of them didn't even have to carry water from the lake. That was a woman's work. A man fished or trapped or took an occasional job in the mine. The rest of the boys Alex's age didn't have to do much of anything. They didn't even have to go to bed unless they wanted to.

Pete could make him take care of the kids or help with woman's work—but only if he found him. The slight, dark-skinned youngster soon learned to recognize the signs of impending assignments and prepared several hideouts nobody knew about.

One was under the back steps. He painstakingly enlarged a little hole to make it possible for him to squeeze through. Given a few seconds warning he could dart out the door and wriggle out of sight before anybody knew he was gone. Another hiding place was beneath a ragged quilt in the old bombardier° rusting away in the yard. He hid in the broken down vehicle dozens of times and Pete never once thought of looking there.

Alex soon learned, however, that it was not enough to have a place to hide. He had to be smart enough to guess when they were about to put him to work, so he would have time to slip away. There were always clues to be read if he kept alert and looked closely enough.

Furtively he watched the level of water in the bucket. Let Pete or his wife start across the rough, uneven kitchen floor or rattle the dipper and he skinned out. Or if a mother approached, her baby strapped in a *takinakan* on her back, he made for one hiding place or another, or simply fled into the woods. When that happened he remained hidden until the family went to bed, even though it meant missing a meal or two.

°A vehicle with a half track on the rear and skiis on the front. It is used for traveling on snow.

Things seemed bad enough while his father was alive. The old man stayed with Pete too. And if Alex was being beaten too hard his father could be depended upon to intervene. Things got worse after sickness hit the settlement the winter Alex was seven. His father died.

About the same time gold was discovered north of the settlement in an area even more isolated than Sachigo. Pete got work there, moving his family to a little shack in the new settlement. They took Alex along.

He looked forward to the move.

"No more taking care of babies," he boasted to his friends. Their eyes taunted him.

"Huh! Pete will make you take care of kids. You'll see."

They had not lived in the new settlement more than a week when he learned that his friends were right.

"Mrs. Morin is bringing her baby this afternoon," Ella said to Alex as they sat at the homemade table eating lunch of bannock and smoked fish. "She wants you to take care of him."

The boy glared at her darkly.

"You run off and I'll tell Pete. He'll whop you good for it."

Alex did not reply and she thought the matter was closed. It was, but not in the way she supposed.

As soon as they finished eating he slipped out of the house and made his way into the woods. He planned on staying nearby, hiding only long enough for Mrs. Morin to come and leave but, restlessly, he made his way through the bush in the direction of the Ricalton cabin. He had met Jim Ricalton, an Indian lad about his own age, a few days before.

Jim was near the house, teasing an injured squirrel with a pointed stick. He looked up as Alex approached, but did not speak. Neither did Alex. Instead he hunkered down beside Jim and watched idly.

"Here, let me."

Wordlessly Jim handed the stick to him. He jabbed the frightened animal in the side, laughing at the squeals of pain.

"Look at 'im jump."

After a time the boys tired of that and threw the stick into the bush. The young squirrel dragged himself painfully away.

"Ever hide from your mum, Jim?" he asked.

"When she's drunk."

Alex considered his answer. He knew a lot of kids who found it wise to hide from their mum and dad when they were drinking. But it wasn't likely that she'd be drunk now. It was a week until payday at the mine and two weeks until family allowances came. There would scarcely be a bottle left in the whole settlement. Jim's mum wouldn't be drinking, so he wouldn't have any excuse to run away for awhile.

Nevertheless Alex eyed him hopefully. "Anything doing around here?"

Jim shrugged his shoulders. "Nothin' except playin' with the squirrel and you let him get away."

The corners of Alex's mouth lifted. "I know some place we could go."

"Where?"

"Let's go to the mine."

Jim sucked in his breath sharply.

"What's the matter? You scared?"

Jim hesitated, fear clouding his eyes.

"There's nothin' to be scared of." Alex's lips curled his derision.

"Scared?" He got to his feet. "I'll show you if I'm scared or not." He started resolutely toward the trail.

A heavily loaded ore truck pounded past as Jim and Alex reached the road connecting Sachigo Mine with the mill and airport. Dust swirled about them.

"It's a long walk to the mine."

"Who said anything about walking? We'll hop a truck."

It was several minutes before a slower vehicle lumbered past.

"Come on, Jim!" Alex screamed as the big truck negotiated the corner. "Let's jump!"

The diminutive seven-year-old waited until the truck was

almost past so the driver wouldn't see him. Then he sprinted out of the bush, caught hold of a heavy brace and swung nimbly up on the big steel box.

Jim started at the same time, but when he reached for the brace his courage failed and he fell back. Triumphantly, Alex grinned and waved at him.

3

Just before the truck turned in at the mill where the gold was refined Alex jumped off, rolling in the dirt. Quickly he scrambled to his feet and looked about. No one had seen him, he realized thankfully. At least no one paid any attention to him.

He looked about. This gave promise of more excitement than caring for kids or teasing a squirrel. And he wouldn't have to worry about Pete or Ella pouncing on him.

Stealthily he came out from behind the little frame building and approached the place where the truck was dumping. Now this was interesting. A conveyor belt two hundred yards long was lifting ore from the stockpile on the ground to the top of the crushing house as high as an average jack pine.

If a fellow had the nerve he could ride almost to the top. That would be a thrill. Alex weighed his own courage, jerked erect and edged cautiously in the direction of the conveyor.

He moved so slowly the men working nearby took no notice of him.

A dozen feet from the lower end of the belt he stopped, transfixed by the daring of what he was about to do. Then in a sudden, impetuous move he dashed across the rocky ground and bounded nimbly onto the belt. Up he went, heart thumping against his rib cage. Alex started to jump, but he could not. Fear held him motionless.

"You, kid!" the foreman shouted hoarsely from just outside the office door. "Get off there!" His profanity roared above the clattering of machines.

Frozen, Alex stared into the dark inwards of the rock crusher as he moved up. Somebody ran to stop the belt and the foreman shouted again.

At the last instant the boy jumped.

Landing on his feet he scurried away like a frightened rabbit. The terrified foreman's yell faded into the background noise. A safe distance from the mill Alex stopped, breathing heavily. It was some time before he could grin again. That ride was a little more than he had figured on. If he'd gone in that building he'd have been chopped to pieces.

Then he remembered the look on the foreman's face. He'd scared him. He'd scared him good. His grin came back and he swaggered a little as he sauntered toward home. The next time he got to the mill he'd scare that foreman again. He'd run him crazy.

When he finally got home Pete was waiting for him, anger constricting the heavy muscles in his face.

"Alex, you didn't take care of the Morin baby this afternoon like Ella told you."

"I thought she said I was to take care of the baby tomorrow," Alex began, innocent brown eyes upturned.

A cuff sent him sprawling.

"I've warned you, Alex! Don't lie to me!"

"But I did." Alex spoke meekly, picking himself off the floor.

24

Another blow upended him.

"I tell you again, don't lie to me," Pete hissed between clenched teeth.

Alex got the beating so he wouldn't lie again, or so Pete warned. But it didn't work that way. It only made him more cautious and clever; more adept at outwitting them. He soon learned which stretches of road slowed the ore trucks enough so he could hook a ride. He discovered that the second or third ride on the conveyor belt wiped away his fear of it. And he found out how far from the belt the foreman had to be before he could get to it and be carried out of reach.

He learned that the hard way—by getting caught and whipped with a willow switch until thin stripes of blood crisscrossed his thin buttocks. But in spite of that it was fun to hang around where the men were working.

He discovered that the second shift came up at seven o'clock to eat lunch and that they were suckers for a pained expression and a story that was told with the proper amount of emotion. For a time he would hang back, watching the men eat. At last they would become aware of him and he would move closer, lips trembling.

"Are you going to eat *all* your lunch?" he asked plaintively.

An approach like that worked better than outright begging.

"Are you hungry?"

"I'm not so hungry now." His lips trembled. "I had a little something to eat last night."

When that didn't bring something to eat he went on to tell them about Pete being drunk and beating him. That story was also good for getting him a place to stay for the night. The women knew about such things. If they didn't have to endure such treatment themselves, they knew many others who did.

Alex could beg more than he could eat from the men on the second shift, but it was more fun to steal it, once he learned that they kept their lunches in the shed. There was excitement with it and he got more variety. Besides, that way he could

25

eat any time. He didn't have to wait until they came up to eat.

Alex went home or not, as the mood seized him. Pete railed at him and beat him soundly every now and again, but he didn't get much work out of his youngest brother unless Alex had a mind to work—and he usually didn't.

Then one day Pete stumbled onto the boy in an Indian family's home. He grabbed Alex by the collar and gave him the worst beating he had ever had. After that Alex was more wary than ever. If he could see Pete coming first, his brother didn't have a chance. He could wriggle under a building, dart into another cabin or sneak around the sheds or trucks in seconds. He was like a mink when it came to slipping away.

One day toward the end of the summer, Alex's vigilance lapsed. He didn't see Pete coming until his brother was a dozen paces away.

Alex whirled and dashed in the opposite direction, but he was too late. Triumphantly Pete dove for him, clamping a hand about his ankle.

"I got you this time!" he exclaimed.

Alex struggled to get away, but Pete tightened his grip.

"You come with me, Alex!" he panted. "We're going to cut wood this afternoon."

The boy grimaced. "That hurts!"

By this time his older brother was again on his feet.

"You run away from me one more time and you'll find out what hurts!" Pete warned, giving him a shove that almost sent him sprawling.

Alex knew when he was beaten.

"OK," he said. "OK. I'll go along."

"I've already wasted two hours hunting for you." His brother pushed by and strode angrily up the road.

Angry that he had been so careless he permitted himself to be caught, and still defiant, Alex hung back. It was two miles to the place where Pete was cutting firewood, and the day was hot. Pete could walk if he wanted to. Alex wasn't walking

26

all that distance if he could help it. He paused and looked down the road. An ore truck was coming.

The boy's eyes gleamed. That was good luck. He'd hop the truck and beat his older brother to the woodlot by twenty minutes. Pete would think he had given him the slip again.

Grinning impishly, Alex slunk off the road with such stealth Pete didn't even miss him. He sought a spot between two small frame buildings where he could not be seen and waited. Moments later the truck rumbled slowly by with several workmen on the back.

Quickly Alex darted out, as he had done so many times before, caught up with the big truck, and grasped desperately for a handhold. But there was nothing within reach. Some boys would have given up at that, but not Alex. Making his way to the opposite side so Pete wouldn't see him by glancing back, he tried to run beside the slow-moving vehicle, his fingers still clawing for a hold.

He almost reached an iron brace when he lost his footing, slipped and fell under the heavily loaded truck. Double wheels ran over his legs.

Alex screamed wildly.

But the men on the truck did not hear him and his brother did not look back.

Sweat beaded his thin young face and his shoulders began to jerk convulsively. The pain surged up into his frail body in great sledgehammer blows.

He screamed again.

Then nausea engulfed him. His vision blacked out, and mercifully, unconsciousness came.

Usually that stretch of road was quite busy. If there weren't ore trucks running from the mine to the mill, people were walking from their homes to the trading post or to work. But on that particular afternoon it was deserted. Half an hour passed before someone came along.

The first Indian to see Alex lying there was almost past when he became aware of the injured boy. He stopped and

27

came back, staring down at Alex's mangled young body. The bronze in his cheeks paled. Hurriedly he turned and rushed on.

Alex was still unconscious when two others came walking by.

"Look! It's that ornery LeLiberte kid."

The man's voice was hushed. "He must be dead."

His companion took a step closer. "He's hurt bad, but I think he still breathes."

He knelt beside the injured boy while the one who was with him raced back to the mine for help.

The young Soulteaux lay motionless in the road. He did not move or make a sound and the look of death was upon him.

By the time he was taken to the hospital Pete and his wife were already there.

"We're going to do the best we can to take care of him here," the doctor explained, "but I'm not sure whether we've got the equipment we need. We might have to send him to Norway House or Kenora."

Alex stirred restlessly and a tortured groan escaped his lips.

Morphine freed the boy of pain throughout the night. As morning came, however, the pain surged back to waken him. Slowly he opened his dark eyes and looked about, bewildered by the strange, unfamiliar whiteness of the little room.

He remembered nothing that happened and was only dimly aware that he had been hurt. He pulled in a long, deep breath and tried to move. The effort was enough to send pain sweeping over him in great, pounding waves. Sweat came out on his neck and face again and his stomach churned until he was sure he was going to vomit. A strange dizziness seized him and for an instant his vision blurred.

All day he drifted between sleep and wakefulness. Dimly he remembered seeing someone standing over him. Once he thought he recognized Ella's voice, but he lapsed into unconsciousness again, and by the time he wakened an hour or so later he had completely forgotten it.

He remembered the doctor. He was the one who jabbed

28

him with a needle when the pain was about to become unbearable. And the nurse who spoke so softly he could not understand her. There was tenderness in her voice and in the gentle touch of her hands.

Time had never meant very much to Alex. He ate when he was hungry, slept when he was tired and, if he could escape Pete and Ella's clutches, he played the days away. In the hospital time meant even less. Days were divided into periods of sleep and wakefulness, interspersed with great crescendoing bouts of pain. How long he was there he didn't know. Nor did he care. However, he gradually began to have less pain. And as it diminished so did the periods of sleep.

When he was feeling better the medical staff studied the X rays of his mangled legs and decided to send him out for treatment. He was flown first to Norway House, and then to Kenora, Ontario, where he was taken to the Catholic hospital.

Now that the pain had ceased he didn't mind the hospital so much. At least there wasn't any water to fetch or babies to take care of. And he didn't exactly miss Pete and Ella, although they did seem to feel bad that he had been hurt.

They put casts on both of his legs and it was months later before he was able to walk around the halls.

Alex sized up the hospital expertly. It wouldn't be much of a job to run away from this place, he reasoned as he looked about him. The Sisters were easier to fool than Pete had ever been. They believed anything he told them. All he would have to do was watch his chance and beat it when nobody was looking.

It wasn't the hospitals or the nuns that caused him to stay. Kenora was a lot bigger than either Sachigo or Sachigo Mine, and he wasn't acquainted with anyone. It might not be so easy to get something to eat and a place to stay. It was better to stay where he was than run the risk of being cold and hungry.

The day the doctor told him he was going to be released

from the hospital, he also had some other news for him. Someone had come to see him.

Alex's eyes narrowed. Pete wouldn't come all the way down to Kenora just to see him.

The door opened and a slight, balding individual came in. He sat down across from Alex, smiling professionally.

"I'm with the Department of Indian Affairs," he explained.

"I haven't done anything."

"We're quite aware of that, Alex. I've come to tell you that you won't be going back to Sachigo Mine."

The boy stared at him.

"It's been decided that you'll go to the boarding school here in Kenora."

Anger smoked in Alex's dark eyes.

4

Alex was thirteen and had finished the third graa when the agency surprised him by sending him home. His brother Emil, who lived at the isolated mining community of Pickle Crow, wanted him to come and live with him and his wife. There was a school there he could go to, so they sent him north.

Alex left the school willingly. He had only gone because he had to. There wasn't anything in school that interested him. It didn't matter one way or another to him that he had learned to read and write.

He looked forward to going to Emil's. Thelma was quiet and easygoing. She wouldn't care what he did and she wouldn't be making him do a lot of stuff either. She didn't even yell at Emil when he spent half his paycheck gambling or on bootleg whiskey. Living with them might be all right. At least they didn't have as many kids as Pete and Ella had and they wouldn't expect him to take care of half the others in the settlement.

Before getting on the plane he made up his mind about school. He didn't care what that agency white man said. He wasn't going. Not at Pickle Crow or any place else. He'd had all the school he was going to have.

He half expected he would have a little trouble with Emil on that school business. He knew well enough what Pete would have said. But as it turned out Emil didn't much care whether he went to school or not. Emil had his own problems making a living for himself and his family. Alex soon learned Emil's chief concern in him was that they would get his government allowance if he lived with them. When the boy informed him that he had a job sweeping out the village's makeshift hotel and running errands for the manager, he shrugged indifferently.

Alex was the one who was disillusioned. He soon discovered that he didn't like the work very well, even though he received $3.50 a day. On Saturday night his employer wanted him to come back after closing and scrub the floor in the tavern. That was bad enough, but the guys he ran around with didn't work anywhere. They made him feel he was missing something by having a job that kept him busy on Saturday night. At last he could stand it no longer.

"I've got things to do Saturday nights," he said. "I think I'll quit."

The hotel manager eyed him narrowly. "You know, Alex," he said in broken Soulteaux, "some of the miners who come in here on Saturday night get pretty drunk."

The boy nodded. *"Ehe."** He knew that already. He had seen them slobbering in their beer or sprawling drunkenly on the floor.

"Sometimes they lose money on the floor and generally I give the money to the one who finds it." He paused significantly. "So if you're scrubbing the floors it would be yours."

*Yes.

32

Alex considered the hotelkeeper's remark. It wouldn't hurt to hang around one more Saturday night and see what happened. If a fellow picked up enough money off the floor it might be worth staying on the job for awhile.

The next Saturday night he found three dollars in small change scattered among the tables and chairs. He counted it four times. This was more like it. Three whole dollars and he didn't even have to work for it. He waited impatiently for the next Saturday night to come. That time he only found fifty cents and the next a few pennies under a dollar.

It was not until he quit working a year later that he learned the hotel owner had been baiting the floor for him. The boss watched him for signs of restlessness, and whenever it looked as though he was about to quit his Saturday night responsibilities he would scatter a couple of dollars in small change on the floor. If Alex picked up a sizable number of coins he was good for another month or so of Saturday night work without complaining.

Alex got acquainted with many of the miners by working at the hotel. His first Christmas at Pickle Crow a group of them invited him to visit them in their bunkhouse.

"Here, kid," one of them said, "try some of this." He passed him the bottle.

Hesitation gleamed in Alex's solemn brown eyes.

"It'll make a man of you."

He eyed them defiantly. And while they snickered he tipped the bottle high and took a deep draught. Grimly he swallowed, choking against the searing burn in his throat. But he managed to keep them from knowing how it burned going down.

"Say now, you've got to give that kid credit. He's one Soulteaux who's goin' to be able to drink like a man."

Alex didn't like the searing burn in his throat, but the warm glow in his stomach was something else again. That and the strange feeling that came over him that he was just as good and as brave and as strong as anyone else he'd ever met. He had never known a few drinks would do that for a fellow. No

33

wonder most of the men he knew made for the liquor store or the bootlegger every time they got paid. It wasn't long until he was buying liquor himself.

With the prices the white bootlegger charged Indians it wasn't easy to get liquor even while he had a job.

"Fifteen dollars for one bottle of whiskey?" he protested.

"I can't help it. I've got to charge plenty. You don't know the risks I'm takin'."

The boy felt the crumpled bills in his pocket.

"Ain't got no fifteen dollars."

"I can let you have a bottle of wine for half that."

Alex shook his head. "I don't got that, either."

The best I can do is some beer—a dollar a bottle, but I don't make hardly nothin' on it. I just sell it as a favor. You c'n take it or leave it."

Alex thrust three soiled bills into his hands.

He was soon well known by the local bootlegger.

        *   *   *

As Alex's drinking began to attract attention, the manager of the hotel tried to talk to him.

"You ought to be saving your money instead of drinking so much. Maybe you can have your own business someday."

What the white man said had a nice sound to it. Alex turned the words over in his mind after he went to bed and wondered what it would be like to have a business of his own. Maybe he could have a hotel and hire somebody to sweep the floor and run errands for him. He could get somebody to stay behind the desk and take in the money for him. And every once in awhile he could come in and tell the fellow to do something just to see him obey.

But whoever heard of a Soulteaux having a store, let alone a hotel? For the Indian it was the trapline, his nets for fishing, and the money the agency gave to him. It didn't make any difference how hard he worked. He could never have any of the things the hotelkeeper talked to him about.

After a year of working at the hotel he decided to quit.

"That's not good, Alex. You need something to keep you busy."

Defiance blazed in the boy's eyes. He didn't argue. That was not his way. Neither did he stay.

The next couple of years Alex lived by his wits—drinking, gambling, fighting and stealing. He didn't work, but neither did any of his friends. He slept all day and caroused all night. If they had any money they played poker and drank until it was gone.

On one such occasion they sold a bunch of stolen fish and arranged for a game in a cabin near the lake. When Alex got there that evening an attractive young Ojibway girl was sitting at the table.

"Hi," she said.

He pulled up a chair near her and sat down. "I don't think I've seen you before."

"Don't you know her?" John Loon broke in. "I thought everybody knew Lumberjack Mary. She came in with the timber crew a few months ago and liked it so well she wouldn't leave."

Mary L'Assandre's shyness fled. "Shut your big mouth, John, and give me a drink."

Reaching for the bottle, Alex eyed her obliquely. She didn't show it in her speech yet, but she had been drinking quite a lot. That was liquor, not a shy young Ojibway maiden talking. Sober, she would probably only giggle and look away self-consciously. Alex didn't know why, but it bothered him to see her like that. She was as brazen and noisy as a white woman.

It wasn't long until they began to play cards. Alex had a bad run of luck from the first hand he was dealt. He was soon out of money and out of the game. Other times when that happened he left in disgust. Not so this time. He remained at the table, watching the game.

Mary was better at poker than most girls who joined them. She won a few hands before her luck turned. Even though

35

she played a good game she reached the place where she bet her last dollar.

John raised her last bet.

She searched her purse, cursing when she found nothing.

"The best hand I get all night," she fumed, "and no more money to bet. How about mukluks? I just made them." She bent to take them off.

He shook his head. "No mukluks. They'd be too small for me."

"If you win, they'll be good for your wife." Her eyes flashed. "If you win," she added.

"I ain't got no wife."

"No wife?" Her eyes lighted. "If I lose I stay one night with you. How about that, big boy?"

One of the fellows snickered.

John fished a couple of bills from his pocket and slammed them in front of him.

"Two nights."

She studied her cards momentarily.

"Let's see you beat this." He spread the cards face up on the table.

She groaned aloud.

He began to scoop up the money and stuff it into his pocket. "All right, Mary, let's go."

She got to her feet, giggling drunkenly.

Alex put his hands against the table's edge and pushed himself back. This sort of thing usually happened when girls got into their poker games, which was often. Yet it never ceased to revolt him.

✿   ✿   ✿

The time came when Alex was tired of lying around and not having any money. He got a job on the rockcrusher at the mine. That was where he was working the following fall when his cousin Mathias Morris came to see him.

It had been more than a year since he had seen his cousin

36

and he was anxious for his company. He invited him to share his crude little cabin.

"Maybe for tonight. I want to talk to you."

Alex squinted at him appraisingly. "Yeah?"

Mathias said no more for a time. Alex lifted one corner of the mattress on the floor and reached for his only bottle of whiskey. He didn't like sharing it when he was almost broke and it was still a week until payday, but Mathias had shared his whiskey with him. So he could do no less.

"Have a drink."

His cousin shook his head. "I don't feel like having a drink."

Alex tipped the bottle to his lips and set it back on the table. It wasn't like Mathias to turn down a drink. He enjoyed his liquor as much as anyone else. There must be something wrong.

Still Alex did not press his guest. Mathias would speak of the things that troubled him when the time came. Mathias talked with Alex about the trapping and the price of furs and the commercial fishing that was due to begin at Sachigo in a few months.

At last his guest fell silent. And Alex could tell that he was about to reveal the purpose of his visit.

"Anything wrong, Mathias?"

"Yeah." Painfully the admission dragged from his lips. "I've just come from McFarland."

Alex's eyes lighted. That was where his mother's people lived.

"Did you see Theodore Tobias?"

"Yeah, I saw him."

"Is he well?"

"Yeah." Mathias fought to make the words come out. "He did the 'shaking teepee' while I was there."

"The shaking teepee?" Alex gasped. Ever since he was a boy on his father's knee he had heard about the shaking tee-pee. How only the witch doctors with great powers could summon the evil spirits necessary for such demonstrations.

37

How strange and terrifying things were done through the shaking teepee.

"Yeah?" He leaned forward eagerly. "What was it like, Mathias? Did it make your heart stand still? Did it turn your blood to water? Did it make you afraid?"

Mathias did not reply to the younger man's questioning. Instead his voice lowered to a hoarse whisper.

"Has somebody put *nisenimow*† on you, Alex?" he demanded. "Has somebody hexed you?"

Terror leaped to his dark, brooding features. He took another quick drink, slammed the bottle back on the table, and wiped his mouth with his sleeve.

"Did Theodore say I have a hex on me?" he croaked miserably. "Did he say I am hexed?"

Mathias shook his head. "He didn't say you have a hex. He didn't say you don't. He only said the spirits talk to him about you."

Alex gasped.

"He said they sent a message to you, Alex. They want you to know what will happen."

Involuntarily he reached for the bottle, but to his stomach the whiskey was like water, flat and impotent, powerless against the growing fear within him.

Mathias struggled for words. "He said he saw you in his shaking teepee trance. He said that bad things will happen to you, Alex. A lot of bad things. It scares him to even think about them."

Sweat moistened Alex's bony fingers as he reached once more for the bottle. He moved as though to take another drink but changed his mind and went to return it to the table. In his agitation he knocked the bottle to the floor and broke it. The stench of cheap whiskey filled the dirty little cabin. Alex groaned his dismay, but made no move to clean up either the broken glass or the liquor. He stared fixedly into Mathias' somber eyes.

†A spell or hex.

"What did he say would happen?" Alex wanted to know, his voice quavering.

Mathias spoke hesitantly, as though the very speaking of the words might make them come true. "You'll get real sick, maybe."

"Sick?" He had been sick once and in the TB Sanatorium for months. Maybe the dread tuberculosis was going to come back.

"Maybe you will cut your foot with your ax in the woods and die before help comes. Maybe the wind will turn your canoe over while you're fishing." His tense voice lowered to a whisper. "Or maybe the wolves will get you on your trapline."

Nervously Alex squirmed in the crude, handmade chair. His breath came in short, quick stabs.

"Did Theodore say I would die?" It was all he could do to speak the dread word.

Mathias moistened his lips uneasily. Almost imperceptibly he nodded.

"He said I should come and tell you, Alex. He says you should know!"

It wasn't true. It couldn't be. It was some sort of cruel joke. Mathias would start to laugh at any moment and the gang he ran with would come bursting in. They would all laugh about how scared he was and he'd probably have to buy another bottle so they could have a couple of rounds of whiskey.

But it wasn't a joke. The frightened boy could tell as much by looking into his cousin's face. A hex was nothing to joke about. Somebody had put a hex on the friend of his father one time. All winter the evil spirits sprung his traps so he got no beaver or mink or muskrats. And when he went hunting they drove the moose and deer away, even before he knew they were there. At last he had been forced to give up his trapline and go back to the settlement, as lean and haggard as a half-starved wolf.

Mathias said it might not be a hex, but there was small comfort in that. The witch doctor was in contact with the spirits of the future. They *told* him what was going to happen. And he said they prophesied that Alex was going to die.

His slender frame shook.

"What can I do now, Mathias?" he croaked. "What can I do?"

His cousin reached out and picked up a spoon Alex had used to eat breakfast with the morning before. For a time he toyed with it, twisting and turning it in his fingers as though he had never seen anything quite like it before. Finally he looked up.

"I've been thinking about that, Alex," he said. "You know, I'm sort of a witchie too. Maybe I can help you."

Hope gleamed desperately in the boy's black eyes.

"You help me, Mathias." He spoke eagerly. "I'll give you what I've got. I'll pay you good. Real good."

But his cousin shook his head. "No pay, Alex. I won't take your money." He paused for the space of a minute or more while Alex waited breathlessly. "But I'll do what I can for you. I'll take care of you for two—three years, maybe."

Gratitude flooded the younger Soulteaux's brown face.

"I'll never forget this, Mathias. Never have I had a better friend than you."

Mathias' expression was still serious.

"My power is not so good as a regular witch doctor like Theodore. I don't do the shaking teepee to get in touch with *those* spirits. I can take care of you two or three years. Then—" He shrugged his shoulders expressively.

Alex's strength drained from him and the color fled from his cheeks leaving them ashen. At first he had misunderstood Mathias. He thought his cousin was powerful enough as a witchie to fix things for him. But now he realized that he had been wrong. For two or three years the bad things, whatever they were, would be kept from him by the witch power of his cousin. Then it would be exhausted and the bad things would come.

In two or three years he would die!

5

Mathias spent the night with Alex, but neither of them slept much. They talked about the old ways and Theodore Tobias, who could commune with the spirits, who could see visions and transmit messages without radios or letters or anything.

"Maybe I can go see him," Alex suggested uneasily. "Maybe I can get him to take away the hex. Maybe if I pay him he will destroy it."

Mathias shook his head. "Theodore talked to me about that. He says he tried to do something right away, but the spirits that told him couldn't do anything with those who make trouble for you." His voice broke. "They are very bad spirits, Alex, and so powerful!"

Alex rubbed his throat thoughtfully. If the spirits were so strong Theodore could do nothing with them, it was small wonder that Mathias feared to tackle them. There were few witch doctors among the Soulteaux who could perform greater wonders than Theodore.

"You think you can keep the spirits from hurting me?" Alex asked, doubt tinging his voice.

"Yeah. For two or three years, maybe. No more. Our uncle showed me tricks that might work. He told me what to look for in the bush. He said which spirits I should talk to." Mathias stopped suddenly. "I think maybe I can do some good for you."

But that was of little comfort to Alex. He had scarcely started to live, it seemed, and already the spirits said he was to die in two or three years. He stared beyond his cousin and out into the ominous darkness of the night.

What would it be like to die?

The next morning Mathias said good-bye gravely and was on his way. Alex remained motionless in the center of the little log building, staring after his cousin. When Alex was finally alone he directed his attention to the broken bottle and the big stain on the floor where the whiskey had washed much of the dirt away and had bleached the rough planks. He *would* have to break his last bottle and there was no money to buy another. He sucked in a quick breath. Right now he needed a drink more than he ever had.

His rifle was standing in the corner, half hidden by some old clothes. It wasn't an expensive gun, but it shot straight and he'd used it to kill his share of game. And he was a good customer of the bootlegger. Maybe he could talk him into letting him have a bottle and hold the gun as security.

Alex started out the door, rifle in hand. A dozen steps from the cabin he hesitated. For a moment he fought with himself, then took it back and set it in the corner. Maybe a man shouldn't think about drinking if he was going to die soon.

Alex should have gone to work that day, but he didn't. He went down by the lake for awhile, walked alone across the settlement in the direction of the mine and, late in the afternoon, he stopped at Emil and Thelma's. They asked him to stay for dinner.

He didn't want to be with them, yet he couldn't stay alone. Not when it got dark again. So he sat in the house talking with Emil. There was a matter that was on his mind—one he had been thinking about ever since he had said good-bye to Mathias. A matter that raced questioningly through his mind.

"Do you go to church?" he asked at last.

"Sometimes."

"Do you go through the learning?" he asked. "Did you have the classes by the minister when you were so high?" He measured the height of a twelve- or thirteen-year-old youngster with his hand.

"Yes," Emil replied. "All the older kids go to the lessons at the Anglican church."

There was a long silence.

"How does a person get to heaven?" There! It was out! He looked at Emil and then away, as though he was only curious about the answer and it didn't matter very much.

Emil considered the question. "He has to do good things," he began uncertainly. "That I remember. Then there should be no gambling, stealing or drinking."

On the inside Alex died a little. He had done those things so much they had become a way of life to him.

"But if he's bad almost all his life," he persisted, "what happens then?"

His older brother frowned and shook his head. "I don't think it's very good for him. Probably it's pretty bad."

It was even worse than he had thought. "You mean he would *never* be able to get to heaven?" Alex's desperation increased.

"That I am not so sure about. If he is good at the very last, if he is very good, then maybe he can make it." However, doubt still weighted Emil's voice.

Alex caught it immediately. A fellow like him who had done bad things ever since he could remember would have a hard time making it into heaven unless his life changed and he lived long enough to pile up many good things to his credit. He only had two years—or three at the most until death would come. With the kind of a life he had been living, he knew where he'd be going.

"I think maybe I'll quit my job," he said with a suddenness that surprised himself. "I think maybe I'll go back to Sachigo."

His older brother eyed him curiously. "Why?"

Alex didn't reply. He was not quite sure just why he wanted to go back to Sachigo, except that he knew he had to.

As soon as possible he left Pickle Crow and returned to his home settlement. His brothers in Sachigo were glad to see him, but there was no work there. Not even for those who had lived there long enough to know everybody.

"Maybe I'll go trapping," Alex said.

"We'll go along," Jonah replied. "Maybe Zacchaeus and I can make a few dollars, OK?"

Trapping would be good, he reasoned. There was nothing to drink out in the bush. He could get started on those good things right away.

They had to wait a week before the ice on the lake was thick enough to travel on. Then a blizzard roared in from Manitoba to dump eighteen inches of snow in the bush and pile mountainous drifts on the lake. At last, however, the weather cleared and they set out with two skinny dogs of uncertain ancestry pulling their toboggan.

It was a day's journey to the trapper's shack where they were going to stay. They had to push the snow away from the heavy plank door to get in.

Zacchaeus was the first to enter. He strode across the magazine-littered floor and leaned over the lone bedstead in the opposite corner to shove aside the faded rag that served as a curtain for the cabin's only window.

Alex took off his snowshoes, stood them beside the door, and stooped to enter. A stale, musty odor pinched at his nostrils, but he scarcely noticed it. He opened the airtight heater,

44

stuffed in some paper and a little kindling, and lit a match. In a couple of minutes the tin stove was rattling noisily as the roaring flames inside gasped for more air. Jonah went over, closed the draft slightly, and shut down the damper to tame the fire.

The following morning they went out to set their traps. Jonah watched Alex fumble clumsily with the first trap. Scorn twisted the older LeLiberte's face as he took it from him.

"Who taught you how to set a trap, Alex?"

"You don't learn to set traps scrubbing floors in beer parlors," he said, grinning good-naturedly.

"Well, somebody better teach you or you'll starve."

All three of them worked at setting the traps. The next day, however, Jonah and Zacchaeus stayed inside. Alex grew restless. A man had too much time to think if he wasn't busy. Taking his rifle Alex went into the bush looking for moose or woodland caribou. The snow was deep and, although he wore snowshoes, the going was slow and tiring. He saw nothing except tracks a week old. When he got back to the cabin just as it was beginning to get dark, the muscles in his legs ached.

Jonah kept saying the trapping and hunting was going to be better after they'd been there a few days, but Zacchaeus was pessimistic.

"I think we'll be lucky to get one fur."

Alex was silent.

Perhaps this was what Theodore Tobias meant when he said something bad was going to happen to him. Maybe the spirits were first going to keep him from getting any game or furs. Maybe the spirits were going to play with him like a cat plays with a mouse before they destroyed him.

He got to his feet and padded silently to the stove in his worn mukluks. Waiting for the spirits to strike was worse than going through whatever ordeal they had for him.

Or so it seemed.

He turned to the frost-rimmed window and stared out into the growing darkness. For two or three years Mathias was

45

supposed to take care of him. He had given his word. But Mathias was only a sort of a witchie. Perhaps it took more power than he had.

What then?

If that was the case how much time did he actually have here on earth?

Somewhere in the distance a wolf howled mournfully. Alex shuddered.

Those who knew about the old ways said that Windigo, the evil spirit, walked in the form of a wolf when there was some major evil to be taken care of. His eyes widened. That was probably no wolf at all, but Windigo out there howling so Alex would know he was there—so he would know there was no way for him to escape.

That night he lay, open-eyed and trembling, staring up at the low ceiling. Occasionally he would feel the room begin to cool and stumble out of bed to stoke the fire. He should have brought a Bible or an Anglican prayer book with him to take to bed. Everybody who knew anything about witch doctors and the hex they could put on a person said that even Windigo was powerless to harm anyone who had a holy book with him.

He half expected the dread evil spirit to strike him down during the night. When nothing happened he felt a little better.

It was two days later when Zacchaeus came home with a scrawny snowshoe rabbit he had caught in a snare.

"Look," he said, laughing to mask his concern. "It's not even good feed for the dogs."

"The dogs aren't goin' to get him," Jonah retorted. "I tell you that."

Seventeen-year-old Alex said nothing to his brothers about Mathias and Theodore and the dread pronouncement of the spirits. Yet he could not think of anything else. He went to sleep with it lying icily in the pit of his stomach or rising up in the window like an apparition to mock him. In the morning he awoke with it knifing painfully into his mind.

To be sure, Alex was not drinking. There had been nothing

for him to drink since they left Sachigo. But the longing was there. He awoke at night dreaming of liquor, savoring the taste of it, calling to mind again the warm glow it brought, and the pleasant release from fear. He wasn't drinking now, but what would happen when he got back to the settlement? He dreaded to think of it.

The older LeLiberte brothers set their traps with all the skill their father had taught them and helped Alex as best they could. He seemed to learn rapidly, but they couldn't be sure. Even the most skillfully prepared set remained empty. For the first time Jonah began to show discouragement.

"Two 'rats and a beaver. Not much for a month's work."

Alex rolled a cigarette. "How long has it been since we've had enough to fill our bellies?"

Zacchaeus laughed mirthlessly.

"We'll have to do like the bears do—go to sleep and live off our fat."

The days wore on endlessly.

Now and again the men managed to get a squirrel or a small spruce grouse or a rabbit. But the snows kept coming, one after another, and the game seemed buried under them. At least there was nothing to be seen, although the brothers hunted with growing desperation from dawn to dark.

It was the same on the trapline. They had been away from Sachigo six or seven weeks when they finally caught a young beaver. The fur wasn't the best, but it did provide them with a few meals.

Then they were out of meat again.

Next they ran out of flour and baking powder for bannock, and had to save their tea leaves to boil them again. When Jonah came in from the trapline that afternoon dejection darkened his solemn face.

"What do you think, Zacchaeus?" he asked, peeling off his heavy parka and advancing to the stove to warm himself. "Will it do any good to stay longer?"

Jonah had been the optimist, the one who looked on each new day with fresh enthusiasm and hope.

"We'll work our traps one more time," Zacchaeus replied. "If we don't catch anything, I think we should go home."

There was nothing in their traps the next time they worked them, but Alex did manage to snare another half-starved rabbit. Zacchaeus cooked it for breakfast to give them strength enough to get back to Sachigo.

6

During the spring and early summer work came hard in the isolated little settlement the LeLiberte brothers called home. The trappers came in off their traplines with the melting of the snow and there was nobody in the village buying fish.

Shortly after the ice breakup, Hudson Bay hired a few of the more industrious to cut and pile wood for seasoning. But that work was finished and the wages spent. Business at the company store dropped off as the credit of one man after another was stopped. Homemade boats dabbed a brilliant scarlet or green or orange were pulled up on shore out of reach of the sometimes angry waves, their gas tanks empty. They would be roaring about the lake again as soon as the monthly government checks came in and their owners could buy gas, but now the boats were useless.

The young men of Sachigo went out hunting when they

49

could scrounge ammunition, gambled endlessly, and slept the mornings away. Few of them had more than a dollar or two in their pockets.

However, Alex was unconcerned.

Not having money was something of a bother when there was a hot poker game going on, or when he felt the urge to buy another bottle. Other than that an empty pocket was no major disaster. After all, he had three brothers and a dozen other relatives living in the settlement.

When Jonah and Sarah Jane ran short of food or got so tired of him they starved him out, he could move in with Zacchaeus or Pete, sharing their bannock and moose meat and smoked fish, and helping eat their macaroni.

Custom would not let them throw him out. Custom and the fear that one day they too might have to move in with someone else who was having a better run of luck than they were.

It wasn't all moose tongue and macaroni living at Jonah's, even though the food and the bed were free. Sarah Jane gave him the same ugly barb of her tongue that she gave to his older brother, and eyed him with that same disapproving stare. The only difference was that Alex didn't have to listen.

"You get a job, Alex," she scolded. "Go to work."

He did not argue with her. Neither did he allow her words to affect his thinking. After all, what did a woman know about work? That was a man's business. If she had her way he and Jonah would be doing something all the time. They wouldn't have an hour to themselves.

And why wouldn't Jonah work? Anything was better than staying around the house listening to Sarah Jane.

"Talk, talk, talk," he murmured under his breath. "Like a noisy little squirrel."

"What did you say?"

He went outside. There ought to be a card game around somewhere, or a bottle that wasn't empty.

When he came back a couple of hours later Sarah Jane was still mumbling to herself. Alex went in and sat down. Staying

50

with Jonah was OK but he was going to have to move soon. He had seen Sarah Jane get that way before. When she did, things had to happen.

The next morning he got up later than usual and slipped into the kitchen. He thought he was going to get his smoked fish eaten and be gone before she got back from the lake with a pail of water, but he was still at the table when she came in.

Snapping brown eyes glared at him. She turned away at first, as though she was not going to speak to him, but she changed her mind and came over to the table, her eyes boring into his.

"We don't have anything for the baby to eat."

Alex did not look up.

"Other people eat the baby's food," she continued, her voice as hostile as her eyes. "His little belly is almost empty."

The baby really wasn't that hungry. Alex could tell by the way he whimpered in the *takinakan*. His little brown cheeks were almost fat, but there was another message Sarah Jane was conveying. He understood it as well as though she shouted it at him. He understood it again when he went to the macaroni pot on the stove that night and saw that it was almost empty, and the next morning when she put a thin wedge of bannock and half a cup of tea before him.

She didn't ask him about leaving. She didn't have to. His growling stomach kept reminding him of it the rest of the day.

Before supper Alex moved in with his brother Zacchaeus.

His brother cornered him in the kitchen. "It isn't good for you to lay around all the time, Alex," he said sternly. "You should get a steady job."

The boy shrugged indifferently. He had been expecting something like this from Zacchaeus. He had thought out his answers.

"There's no work in Sachigo." Besides, a job would interfere with his gambling and drinking and chasing girls. "There's no work in Sachigo," he repeated.

"Go somewhere else. Get a steady job."

That was something Alex had been giving considerable thought to. He had stayed at Sachigo quite awhile—for him. True, he and his friends had been having a wild time when he and his brothers quit trapping, but lately even that had begun to lose its luster. Getting drunk wasn't the fun it once had been and playing cards with the same bunch was old stuff. The girls would be all right, but they soon tired of a fellow without any money.

But Red Lake was different. At least a little work could be found in the gold mining town. He could make a few bucks if he wanted to, and find plenty of girls and whiskey to spend the money on. Red Lake was a place where he could really have himself a time.

Or Kenora. It had been two or three years since he had been there. It might change his luck to go south for awhile.

There was another possibility that was even more intriguing. He could forget going south and get a job fishing commercially. Maybe that was what he ought to do. He could find somebody who was working so far back in the bush that there wouldn't be any temptation to drink. If he was ever going to, he ought to start building up good things so he'd have some sort of a chance of getting into heaven when the witch doctor's solemn pronouncement came true.

At the thought of the witch doctor Alex's belly knotted and fear swept over him. Two years wasn't long to live. Already six months had gone by since Mathias brought him the dread prediction. Before he knew it the two years would be up and his cousin's power as a witchie would be exhausted. In two years he would be dead.

That night Alex stole a bottle of liquor and drank himself to insensibility. But when he awoke he was as miserable and confused as before.

He did not immediately make up his mind to leave Sachigo. For one thing there wasn't any way to the outside without having money to pay for transportation. For another, living with Zacchaeus was getting better.

52

His brother was a little more careful than most. He applied his government check to his bill at the Bay store and was able to get credit again. At his house there was plenty of macaroni and bannock and tea for everyone. A single gill net kept them in smoked fish, and Zacchaeus had the good fortune to kill a moose. Life had never been better at his house.

Alex considered that carefully. A fellow didn't walk out on that sort of eating unless he had to.

But word of the kill spread and their relatives poured in to share the meat. When Zacchaeus finished parceling it to those who came there was little left. His wife's good nature changed at the same time. Not long afterward the size of the meals began to dwindle.

The time had come for Alex to move, so he went to Pete's house. It had been bad staying at Pete and Ella's when he was younger, but now it wasn't so bad. He was welcome there longer than with anyone else. The only thing that really bothered him was Pete's stubborn insistence that he knew what was best for everybody, especially for Alex. Two days after Alex moved in to his oldest brother's house Pete gave him a lecture about leaving Sachigo.

"Jonah says you're thinking about going away, Alex." Disapproval gleamed in his eyes.

"Yeah."

"Going away isn't good for you, Alex. You'd better stay here."

The boy stared at his plate and fought to hold his tongue. The old anger flared hotly, the way it had when he was a boy and Pete ordered him to do a woman's work like taking care of babies or doing dishes. That was the trouble with Pete. He had to boss all the time. It made Alex burn inside.

A week later a float plane landed at Sachigo on the way to nearby Bear Skin. A friend who had been talking with Alex about leaving brought him the news.

"The pilot's a friend of mine, Alex. He said we can go along, if we want to and it won't cost us nothin'."

Excitement gleamed in Alex's eyes. That settled the matter. He wasn't staying in Sachigo to have Pete boss him any longer.

He thought he would be able to slip away without anyone knowing about it, but Pete heard he was going on the plane and rushed back to the house to see him.

"No," he exclaimed harshly. "You're not to leave, Alex. You stay here in Sachigo where you belong." His youngest brother was silent. "You hear?"

Anger and resentment smouldered in Alex's thin young face. "I hear."

He pushed past his brother and stormed into the house.

Pete stood near the front door, undecided whether to come in or not. Then he turned and walked away. As soon as he was gone Alex went into the room he shared with Pete's boys and hurriedly threw his things into his suitcase. With some of the stealth he used to use in sneaking away from his brother when he was seven years old, he made his way outside and down to the aircraft.

Neither Alex nor his friend knew where they wanted to go, or why. But that did not matter particularly. They were leaving Sachigo. That was the thing they cared about.

At Bear Skin they separated. Alex got a job fishing commercially while his friend stayed in the village. He planned on fishing the balance of the season, but in a few weeks he grew restless, quit work and drifted to Red Lake. It seemed that his old friends had all been waiting for him to come back.

"Alex, come have a drink."

He hesitated.

"Just one drink's not goin' to hurt you."

Hurt him? How could it hurt him? His very being was screaming for it! Hungrily he snatched the bottle and tipped it up.

"Wait a minute!" his host cried. "Don't drink all of it!"

Grinning, he handed it back, much lighter than it was before.

The fight he got into a few weeks later had been over

liquor. At least that was the way he remembered it. It came back to him foggily, in disconnected bits and pieces. He remembered the eight of them splitting a bottle of raw bootleg whiskey and chipping in to buy a couple more.

They must have gone back to the bootlegger's several times, although the trips blurred and ran together until he could not separate them. He seemed to remember one fellow picking up a full bottle and somebody else taking a drunken swing at him.

The next thing he knew the air was filled with fists and everybody was falling over everybody else. That was about the time the RCMP broke it up and arrested them. The fine was a staggering fifty dollars each.

"A lot of good drinkin' money," one of his companions complained.

Alex did not answer him. He had never been arrested before. Maybe this was some kind of warning to him of where his life was taking him. He wasn't piling up any good things to get him into heaven, that was sure. The way things were going, when Mathias' witch powers quit working he would be headed for the other place and there would be nothing he could do to stop it.

"I've got a bottle at my house," one of his friends suggested.

Alex shook his head. "I've got things to do."

He left the group and walked along the wide street to his shack by the river. He scuffed along in the snow, dejection dragging at his moccasined feet.

It was not that he expected much out of life. There was little for him or any of his people to look forward to, save successive seasons on the trapline, commercial fishing and the inevitable government checks.

He supposed he would marry some day, if Pete or one of his brothers could arrange it with the father of a girl his age. The Chipweyan and Cree picked out their own wives, but not the Soulteaux. Their marriages were carefully arranged. A young person could refuse to marry the one picked out for him but the feeling in the settlements was so strong against it that few ever did.

Alex looked out across the bay. Working in the mill wasn't so bad once a fellow got used to it. If the trapping wasn't good when he was ready to settle down maybe he could get a job and— But the witch doctor had changed all of that with his look into the future.

Alex wasn't going to have a chance to do any of those things. He was going to die before he had a chance to accomplish anything.

More dejected than ever, he went into his one-room shack and closed the door behind him. He had a bottle under his mattress, but he didn't feel like drinking. Instead he dropped heavily into a crude, handmade chair and rested his arms on the table.

Was this any way for a man to live who was going to die so soon? The ache inside was so great he was scarcely able to bear it.

* * *

About that time Bob Harmon came to Red Lake looking for fishermen. He knew Alex as a good worker and sought him out.

"I understand you're looking for a fishing job, Alex. Do you want to work for me?"

Alex's eyes narrowed.

"Maybe. Where're you working?"

"Windigo."

Alex's dark eyes gleamed. Windigo was even farther into the bush than Sachigo. There wasn't a permanent settlement there; only a handful of commercial fishermen and an occasional trapper. There wouldn't be much drinking in a place like that. Yes, Windigo would be a good place for him.

7

When Bob Harmon flew in to Windigo with Alex, the fishing was just getting under way. Barney Kennequenash was already there with his family, but he was the first. The rest of the crew would be coming in a few days.

"Alex will be fishing with you, Barney," Harmon explained.

Barney nodded without speaking. He was never one to waste words.

"Get the nets out tomorrow. If the weather holds I'll be back with some more of the crew."

Barney did not speak, even when their white employer was gone. Instead he turned and led the way through the snow and growing cold to the bunkhouse where Alex would be staying.

"Do you like working for Harmon?"

Barney shrugged. "Working for one white man is like working for another," he replied indifferently.

Alex nodded understandingly. That was the way he felt about those queer men from the south who were always in a hurry and expected a fellow to run when he worked for them, as though there would never be another day coming. Working for a white man was a way of making a dollar. Not a very good way, he had to admit, but it was something that had to be done at one time or another.

They went into the unheated bunkhouse and Alex threw his battered suitcase on the hard bed. When he had finished laying the fire and touched a match to it, he turned once again to the one who was to be his fishing companion.

"Is there any liquor here?"

"Not now. If you wanted any, you should've brought it in."

Alex did not reply, but his mind eased a little. If there wasn't any liquor, he couldn't drink. Maybe he could start doing those good things after all.

He ate with Barney and his family that night. He knew Barney from Round Lake where he had gone a few times. Barney was a husky, broad-shouldered Soulteaux whom almost everybody liked. He was a quiet one, it was true, but he didn't drink much and had a reputation for good work habits and honesty. If anybody had a job with some responsibility they went to Barney first. Only if he turned them down did they look elsewhere.

Alex went back to the bunkhouse after supper and went to bed. He didn't like being alone, even for a little while. Especially since Mathias talked to him and he dreamed so often of dying.

He sat on the edge of the hard bed and loosed his mukluks. He should have found himself an "adopted wife" to bring along for the winter. It wouldn't have been much trouble to find a girl like Mary L'Assandre to come up and live with him until spring breakup. Most of them were glad enough to get a warm place to stay where they would have plenty to eat. And Harmon wouldn't have cared. He probably had an Indian "wife" or two in the north himself. Besides, if a fellow had a woman with him he was more apt to stay on the job.

Alex shook his head.

He hadn't looked far enough into the future to bring someone with him, so he would have to be alone for the winter. That was one thing he would take care of next year, he told himself.

The following morning as soon as the sun chased away the darkness Barney and Alex harnessed their dogs to a long toboggan and loaded it with nets, ice chisels and the *sipasikwahikan*, the device they would use in putting the nets under the ice for the first time.

Frost rimmed the matted, fur-trimmed hood on Alex's old parka. Stinging cold bit through his duck trousers and worn mitts as he worked. He had long since grown accustomed to ignoring the cold. It was often present, nagging at his slight body and stiffening his fingers and the heavy muscles in his legs. Determinedly he willed it out of mind, pretending that it no longer existed. He didn't quite get away with it, but it helped make the cold more bearable.

"Ready, Barney?" he asked as he finished harnessing the last dog.

Barney picked up the long whip and his arm went up and forward in one smooth, effortless motion. The supple lash snapped over the heads of the dog team with the crack of a rifle. The dogs leaped forward.

Half a mile out on the lake Barney brought the dogs to a halt and he and Alex set to work. Although they had never set nets together, they both knew exactly what had to be done. Alex took the ice chisel and began to chop rhythmically through the brittle ice. Barney goth the *sipasikwahikan*, or jigger, as the white men called it, and saw that it was in working order. He took off his gloves long enough to tie a light line to it, the line that would be carried under the ice by the strange-looking contraption. By this time Alex had the hole cut and they thrust the jigger into it.

With his right hand Barney pulled the rope attached to the spring-mounted rocker arm. It swung forward and up until the sharp end bit into the underside of the ice. As he eased the pressure on the rope the jigger moved forward. The rocker arm released its hold and dropped down again. He repeated the process expertly and the device moved once more.

At first the young Soulteaux pulled the ropes slowly, but as soon as he determined that the device was working properly he manipulated it so fast that Alex, who was tracing its progress by the sound, had to walk rapidly to keep up with it.

"Far enough," Alex called when they were about a hundred yards apart.

Barney stopped and, securing the lines to keep them from being jerked into the icy water, he joined his companion. Cutting a second hole and removing the jigger was only the work of a few minutes. They fastened the net to the light line that had been pulled under the ice, and it was soon in place.

Once that was done they moved to another location.

And so it went. They were out in the cold all day, not even taking time to eat until darkness drove them back. Working the nets once they were placed would not be so tedious. It was putting them down for the first time that was backbreaking.

Alex went back to the bunkhouse that night, glad for the exhaustion that made each move an effort. When he was tired enough he could go to sleep without spending half the night thinking about the witch doctor and Windigo and the terrible thing that was going to happen to him when Mathias could no longer protect him.

The weather was cold but clear and Harmon brought in more fishermen the next few days. It wasn't long until the camp was operating at capacity. It was a big operation and everything moved with machinelike precision that was bewildering and seemed totally unnecessary to Alex. Each man had a responsibility and the foreman saw that he carried it out.

60

He didn't even consider the way a fellow felt. There were days when Alex didn't feel like fishing—when he wanted to stay in bed for a couple of hours or go off for a moose or a couple of rabbits. Or he might want to put out a few traps, or simply sit by the fire. But he couldn't do any of those things. If the weather was good enough to be out at all, everybody had to work.

Dog teams pulled deep lamp-heated boxes on toboggans to keep the fish from freezing, and the catch was stored in the snow until the plane could haul it down to the filleting plant. It wasn't enough that a fellow had to be out on the ice every day it was fit. When he got back he had to take care of his dogs before he could go in and get warm himself. Oh, yes, Harmon was a fair employer, he had to agree. And he paid better wages than most. But what kind of a man was it who thought more of his dogs than he did of the people who worked for him?

It was hard for Alex to understand anyone who insisted that dogs be cared for so well. As far as he was concerned the only care a dog needed was a jackfish or two, if he had them. If he didn't, they could scrounge for themselves.

There were those things that bothered him about Harmon, but he got used to it after awhile—as used to it as he ever would.

Usually there was no liquor at the fishing camp on Lake Windigo, but every now and then someone would induce the pilot to bring in a few bottles. At first Alex didn't drink with the others, but it wasn't long until he was clawing as thirstily for his share as anyone else.

The following October the fish plane brought Alex and his bunkhouse companion a couple of fifths of whiskey. The plane was scarcely in the air again when they finished the first and began to squabble over the second. Alex took a long drink and staggered to his bunk. The next thing he knew it was morning.

Miserably he swung his feet over the side of the bunk and

sat up. The pain in his head was as nothing compared to the aching in his heart. Time was running out. The day when Mathias' witchcraft powers would be exhausted was racing nearer and nearer. Before he knew it there would be no more help for him and the witch doctor's prediction would come true. The way he was still living he knew there wouldn't be any question about where he would go.

Alex went to the window and looked out at the powdery snow that was sifting to the ground. He was supposed to be getting better and better, but he wasn't. He was getting worse. There were no good things counting for him in heaven, that was for sure. Nothing that could keep him from going to the bad place where nobody wants to go.

Not long afterward his companion who lived in the bunk-house quit and a new fellow from Red Lake came to take his place. When he finished unpacking Alex saw that he had put a Cree Bible on the makeshift table in the corner. He had seen one once before, but he couldn't remember where. Curiously, Alex watched, but he never saw the stranger pick up the Bible. The dust began to thicken on the cover as the days passed.

From time to time Alex sauntered over and looked at it, wishing he knew what was inside. The Bible was a holy Book, he had heard men say. Some claimed it could keep the evil spirits from hurting a fellow. All he had to do was take it to bed with him and he would be safe.

He picked up the Bible wistfully and thumbed its pages. He knew the Cree syllabics well enough to read a little.

If a book like this could keep the evil spirits from hurting a person while he slept, maybe it could help him do good instead of bad things. He sat down and, opening the Bible at the front as they taught him to read books in school, he began to sound out the words. It was slow, painful going, but he kept at it.

Not until the door opened and his bunkmate stepped inside did he realize what he was doing. Flushing, he looked up and closed the Book quickly. But the fellow didn't seem to be aware of what he was doing. He shuffled across the rough floor, stirred the fire with a short iron rod and slouched in a chair nearby.

After that Alex read the Bible from time to time. He tried to force himself through a chapter every night. There were nights when what he read made sense and he was gripped by the stories. Other times he got caught in a tangle of unfamiliar names of peoples and towns and countries. On those occasions despondency took hold of him.

He was going to quit reading the Bible, he told himself, throwing it carelessly on the table after one such bewildering session with it. There wasn't any use in trying to study it out when he couldn't understand it. In spite of himself, however, he kept going back to the Bible, drawn compulsively to it.

One afternoon when they finished fishing he was sitting alone in the bunkhouse reading when Barney came in.

"What are you reading?" Curiosity tinged his voice.

Wordlessly Alex held up the Bible.

"Do you understand it?" There was awe in Barney's voice.

Alex shook his head.

His friend got a chair and sat down near the stove. Winter was only beginning, but already the cold was increasing steadily with each passing day. One day the snow would be four feet deep.

"You know," Barney continued after so long a time Alex all but forgot what they were talking about, "I saw an old friend from Round Lake the other day. He said there's a new white man in the settlement."

"Oh?" Alex questioned. White men were always coming to one settlement or another. They either wanted to sell poor goods at fantastic prices, get the Indians to work for them for nothing, or take the women. There was nothing new about that.

"He came to tell the people about God," Barney said.

Interest gleamed in the handsome young Soulteaux's face. He made no effort to hide it.

63

"Is he a priest?"

Barney shrugged his indifference.

"Maybe he is. Maybe he isn't. Joe didn't say."

Alex began to talk of other things, but his thoughts were on this white stranger at Round Lake. If this one had come to the settlement to tell the people about God, maybe he was the one to go to for help with his problem. Maybe he could straighten out the tangled words of the Bible and make it speak clear and plain like the voice of a trusted friend. Maybe he could help him start to do good things instead of bad things all the time.

Turning, he glanced at his friend.

"This one at Round Lake who talks to people about God, Barney—" he began.

"Yeah?"

"Will he speak to *anyone* of God?"

Barney's eyes narrowed. "What do you mean, Alex?"

"Is it only the good people he speaks to of God? Would he speak to a bad one about this—this Book?" He indicated the Bible. "Someone like *me?*"

Barney shrugged. "How do I know what another man will do? My friend just said that he came to speak to people about God. That's all."

The ache in his chest continued to grow. A good man would not want to talk to a bad one about God. A good God wouldn't even want to hear about a person like him. And he couldn't blame him. He couldn't even stay sober if there was liquor around. How could he expect the white man to waste time telling him about God?

Alex went through the motions of fixing the fire, but he was so distraught he scarcely knew what he was doing.

The Round Lake white man had come to tell those who were good about this God of the Bible—this One who was so powerful He made the lakes and the fish and the moose and the sun and the night—everything in six days before He even got tired.

64

Alex pulled in a long, deep breath and slowly expelled the air. If only this God would be interested in a person like him!

As the days went on Alex continued to think about the white man at Round Lake. Why would he come all the way to Round Lake to tell the good people about God? If they were good enough, they wouldn't have to hear about Him. It might be worthwhile for him to go to Round Lake and find out.

At night sleep was long in coming. Alex wakened frequently and when he did, his thoughts drifted to this stranger at Round Lake. If only he could talk to him!

A blizzard whistled into Windigo a week after Alex talked with Barney. And with it, trouble piled on trouble. For two or three weeks the weather was so foul the plane could not come in. The boxes of fish increased day by day.

Bob Harmon chafed impatiently for the weather to clear so he could start moving fish again. The moment the snowing stopped and the wind went down Alex appeared at his employer's door.

"Come in, Alex."

Harmon indicated a chair near the wood-burning heater.

"It's good to see the sun shine a bit, eh?"

Alex answered him painfully. He talked about the fishing, and a rabbit he had caught in a snare the day before.

"He was thin, that one," he said, "like a squirrel."

Presently the words stopped coming and he sat, undisturbed by the silence. The white man tapped tobacco into his pipe and sucked on it reflectively. He knew the customs of the Indians well enough to know there was purpose behind the visit. He even surmised what that purpose was. But he waited with the patience of an "Indian man" until Alex got to his feet to leave. Only then did the boy speak his heart.

"The fish plane comes tomorrow, eh?"

"If the weather holds."

The corners of the white man's mouth tightened and his face grew stern.

Briefly fear leaped to Alex's eyes. Fear that he would be

forced to stay and work until the ice went out. Grimly he fought for the courage to voice his request.

"I want to quit," he blurted.

"I need you, Alex. You're the best man I've got."

"But I want to quit now. I've worked for you for a long time."

"Give me one good reason why."

He swallowed hard. "I want to go to Round Lake."

"But that doesn't make sense. I'm paying you as much as anyone else would pay you, even if you could get a job at this time of year—which you couldn't. And you've got a warm place to stay here and plenty of bannock and moose meat and salt pork. Forget this foolishness about quitting and go back to work."

Mutely the Soulteaux boy stood before his employer. How could he tell him about Theodore Tobias and his grim prediction? How could he tell him about the white man at Round Lake who was telling people about God?

The Indian's eyes went round and staring. He struggled for words, but there were none. Tears slipped from beneath his eyelids and made their way down his bronzed cheeks.

Bob saw them and hesitated. For all his gruffness he liked the slight, black-haired lad who stood before him.

"Does going to Round Lake mean so much to you, Alex?"

He nodded.

Briefly the white man remained silent. Then a faint smile lighted his face.

"If you want to go to Round Lake as bad as that, I'll not stand in your way."

8

The heavily loaded Norseman that took Alex to Round Lake angled down to the rough ice. The pilot taxied to a stop near the Hudson Bay dock, leaving the engine idling. Alex looked at him gratefully, scrambled out of the aircraft and got his suitcase. Standing on the hard-packed snow Alex looked toward the settlement.

Round Lake at last! Now he could see the man who knew about God and see if he was willing to talk to a person like him. Maybe the white stranger would be able to help him start to live a good life. It scarcely seemed possible that there could even be a chance of help for him. He had been trying for so long without accomplishing anything. Maybe this one could help him do enough good things so he could go to heaven when Mathias' power ran out and Theodore's prediction came true. His very being trembled.

When Isaac Roy, another cousin, came from the village to see him, Alex was still lost in thought.

"Weren't you fishing for Harmon at Windigo this season?"

Alex nodded.

With that he picked up his suitcase. Snow was beginning to fall again and the trees had started to sough mournfully as the wind came up. The fish-plane pilot revved the engine and taxied into position for takeoff.

Isaac spoke again cryptically. "Fired?"

"Quit."

Hard-packed snow crunched noisily underfoot.

"My wife is at Fort William in the TB sanatorium," Isaac said.

Alex nodded. News has an uncanny way of traveling in the north. For three months he had known that Isaac's wife was in the hospital with tuberculosis. He had known too that her mother was keeping house for Isaac and his children.

"Stay with me."

The slender young Soulteaux hesitated. If he was going to stay away from liquor, this was not the place in the settlement for him to live. Isaac started drinking first and drank longer than anyone else at Round Lake. Even his drinking companions were disturbed by the things he did when he was drunk.

"That crazy Isaac Roy," they used to say, "he's beating his wife again. One day he will kill her."

"Yeah." The speaker nodded sagely. "Nobody at Round Lake is as bad as Isaac."

Isaac headed for his little frame house on the edge of the settlement, taking for granted that his cousin was going to stay with him.

Alex remained silent. It was not good to say bad things to Isaac and make him mad or hurt inside. Better to slip away later in the afternoon without saying anything.

"I show you something, Alex," his cousin began as soon as he took off his parka and hung it up.

Alex frowned. It had been cold coming in the plane from Windigo. To be hospitable was a way of life with the Soulteaux, especially to those of the same family. It did not make for good feelings in his heart to have Isaac want to show him something when his belly longed for a cup of tea and a piece of bannock.

Isaac, however, was not thinking about either custom or food. He returned from the bedroom, his Bible in his hand.

Incredulously Alex stared at him. Isaac with a Bible?

There must be some mistake. He was never one to think about God. He had to have some other reason for bringing out the Book. Maybe he had something hidden in the pages—some money for whiskey squirreled away from the cunning of his wife's mother, or a magazine picture of a white woman without any clothes. Those were the things Isaac went for. Not this Bible with words an Indian found hard to understand.

"Sit down. I'll show you something," Isaac repeated.

Alex sat down at the rough plank table. His cousin pulled up a chair and sat beside him. His fingers were trembling with eagerness as he paged the strange Book.

"Do you know what the Bible says, Alex?" There was wonder in his cousin's voice, as though he had learned some new and marvelous thing. "It says we are all sinners. We need to be saved."

"How do you know this?" Alex asked, awe in his voice. "Did you read it in the Book?"

"Yeah!" He shoved the Bible in front of his younger cousin. "Cooper showed me. He read it just the way God says it. We'll all go to hell unless we confess our sin and—and let this One called Jesus save us."

But Alex was scarcely listening. "This Cooper? Is he the one who came to Round Lake to tell the people about God?"

"Yes!" Isaac's face brightened. "Have you heard of him?"

Alex stared.

"This Cooper, doesn't he *only* talk to good people about God?"

"Oh, no," Isaac retorted quickly. "He says that the Bible teaches that the person who isn't sick doesn't need medicine. He says Jesus didn't come to help the well. He came to take care of the sick."

Alex turned that over in his mind. In a way it didn't seem reasonable that the white man would come all the way to Round Lake to tell bad people about God. Or that God would even want him to. But it didn't seem reasonable either that he would come so far just to talk to good people—people so good they wouldn't need saving—about this God of his.

Alex straightened suddenly. Unless it was as Isaac said and there *weren't* any good people in all the world.

"You mean he talks to those who do bad things? He tells them about God?" This Alex could not understand.

Isaac nodded. "Yeah. He talks to me. I'm a Christian now."

The newcomer's deep brown eyes kindled and he pulled in a long, thin breath. Catholic he had heard. Anglican he had heard. He even called himself Anglican, whatever that meant. But Christian? That was something new.

"What does 'Christian' mean?" he asked curiously.

Isaac frowned and the words were long in coming. These questions from Alex were not easy to answer. All he could say for sure was what had happened to him. He could tell Alex about the bad things he used to do—the bad things he had done when his cousin was in Round Lake the last time. They had gotten drunk together and when they sobered up all their money was gone. These were the things he told his cousin.

"You know what I've been like. I gambled. I drank. I beat my wife until sometimes she was almost sick."

Alex nodded. "Yeah."

Nobody had to tell him about the bad things Isaac had done. With his own eyes Alex had seen him. Alex hadn't liked Isaac much himself. Nobody did. He was a brute when he was drunk and a brute when he was sober. A thief, a liar and a drunken bully.

"Then one day I went to see this Cooper. He talked to me

70

about how Jesus died on the cross to save me and how He loved me so much." Isaac's voice lowered. "All the time I was hurting inside like when I'm sick. It wouldn't go away."

Alex nodded. He had that same feeling after each time he got drunk, only he didn't know anything about Jesus dying on the cross to save him. But the feeling Alex knew well. Just hearing Isaac talk sent it surging through him once more.

"One day I decided I was tired of drink—of living for the devil. I confessed that I was a sinner and put my trust in Jesus to save me. I am a Christian now, Alex."

The younger Indian's thin bronze face remained as expressionless as usual. Yet there was an eagerness in his heart that set him to trembling. If this Jesus could stop Isaac from drinking and fighting and doing bad things, maybe there was hope for him. Isaac had been worse than he had ever been. He drank more, fought more and gambled more.

But perhaps Alex hadn't understood his cousin. Perhaps he didn't mean that he had quit doing bad things.

"You don't drink any more?" he asked.

Isaac shook his head.

"Gamble?"

"Since I have followed Jesus, I don't even want to do those things."

For a long while Alex sat motionless, staring intently at the stove.

"Fight?" he asked. "Beat your wife?"

"I don't beat her anymore. And I haven't had any fights."

Alex considered those things briefly. "And that means you are Christian?"

It was Isaac's turn to ponder. These were things he did not know. He listened and believed when the white man spoke. He even thought he understood when Cooper talked with him. Now the questions of his cousin disturbed him.

"Why don't we go see Cooper."

But Alex was not ready to go and see anyone. He had more questions for Isaac.

71

"How many of these Christians are there at Round Lake?"

"Only me."

That was a disappointment. Alex went on. "If it is so good to be a Christian, Isaac, how is it that you're the only one in the whole village?"

Isaac placed the Bible on his knee and nervously ran his fingers through his shining black hair. It was not easy to answer the questions Alex fired at him. It was not easy even to fight down the doubts they brought to his own mind.

"I talk," he said lamely. "Everywhere I go I talk about what Jesus did for me. But the people don't listen." Again he fumbled with his Bible, uncertain fingers leafing the pages. "I tell them God says we are all sinners and that we don't live the way we should. But nobody will listen."

Alex nodded. He could understand that. The words Isaac spoke were strange to the ear. A man had to ponder them carefully. It would take time probably. There was something else that concerned him more at the moment. His own problem.

"How does that keep you from drinking?" he demanded.

Blankly Isaac's eyes looked past him, as though he had never thought of that before.

"Cooper says God knew we couldn't stop sinning," he went on, "so—"

Suddenly Alex was angry. "I know that I don't live right," he blurted. "And I have trouble with drinking. But how do I stop?"

Isaac stared at his Bible. How could he find the words to explain what was in his heart?

"I stopped," he said simply.

"How?" his cousin persisted.

"I just stopped." He shrugged his shoulders expressively.

Alex did not repeat his question, but it still gleamed in his eyes. This was something he did not understand.

"Maybe we had better ask Cooper," Isaac repeated. This time Alex did not protest.

Alex forgot about finding someplace else to stay. At supper they sat at the table in the kitchen with Isaac's mother-in-law and his two children, eating pemmican and bannock and drinking strong tea. Several young Indian men arrived before they finished eating. Alex studied them curiously.

"Why are they here?" he asked curiously.

"We're going to Cooper's," Isaac explained. "Every night we go there and have him talk to us from the Bible."

Alex made no comment, but secretly he was pleased. Perhaps this white man could say things in a way that he could understand. Perhaps he would put into words how being a Christian could keep a man from wanting whiskey. Perhaps he would explain to a fellow how believing something he had not believed before could keep him from doing bad things so he could go to heaven.

They filed solemnly into the missionary's house. It was sparsely furnished, but to Alex's unsophisticated eyes it seemed a mansion.

And the lamp on the table! It hissed in a way he had never heard a lamp hiss before, and shone so brightly he could hardly look at it. What would it be like to have such a bright lamp? With one of those, the bunkhouse at Windigo would be brighter than the sun.

Cooper had been there only six months. He had not yet learned the language. Usually Isaac interpreted, but for Alex it was not necessary. He didn't understand English well, but he understood enough for him to get by.

"He speaks English," Isaac said, introducing Alex to the white man he had been longing to see. You teach him."

Bible in hand, the gangling, square-jawed missionary patiently explained how sin came into the world. He showed places in the Bible that said all had sinned and come short of the glory of God, and another place where it explained that the wages of sin were death.

Alex nodded somberly. He didn't know about other peo-

73

ple, but he was a sinner. That was sure. And he knew where he was going when he died.

"But how does that help me?" he broke in.

Cooper went on, carefully explaining that God loved him so much He sent His only Son to earth to live a sinless life and die on the cross so Alex could be saved.

That was more difficult for Alex to understand than the things Isaac had told him. Where had God come from before there was any world? And what kind of Father was He to make His own Son die for someone else who didn't even love Him.

Torment twisted Alex's youthful face. He wanted to break in and ask Cooper to explain those things. But that would have been impolite. The intense white man was very friendly and sincere, but he was still a stranger. A Soulteaux was never rude to strangers.

After speaking directly to Alex, Cooper used an interpreter for the rest of the lesson, a verse-by-verse study of the third chapter of the gospel of John.

The study ended far too soon for Alex. He didn't understand much of what the pleasant white man said, but he had a longing to learn more. When he shook hands with the missionary he averted his eyes.

The next morning Alex and Isaac once again turned to the Bible. They had only begun when Alex began to question his Christian cousin.

"Where was God before the earth was made, Isaac? Where did God come from?"

Isaac shrugged. "He was just here. That's all I know."

"But there wasn't any earth," Alex protested.

The question didn't bother Isaac. His was not an inquiring mind. "He *must* have been around someplace."

Alex went on. "What causes you to be saved?"

"Cooper just says it happens. That's all."

The answer was enough for Isaac, but it did not satisfy Alex.

74

He considered the matter briefly and reached for the cigarettes in his shirt pocket.

"If you set a trap," he began, "the spring makes it catch the beaver by the foot. Right?"

"Yeah."

"You go out to chop wood for the fire. You chop the tree and the ax makes it weak until it falls."

He paused, lighted a cigarette and threw the match into the heater.

"Your belly is empty. You eat bannock or pemmican or smoked fish until your belly is full. Then you aren't hungry anymore. Right?"

"That's right."

"You have to set a trap to catch beaver. You have to eat to be full. You have to shoot caribou with the rifle to make mukluks from the hide. There has to be a reason for everything that happens."

Isaac stared at him, uncomprehending.

"If you are saved, something has got to do it," the young Indian repeated. "How does it happen? What is it that makes you saved?"

"Jesus," Isaac said lamely. "He died on the cross."

"But that happened a long time ago. How can it save you now? How can it save me, Alex LeLiberte? That's what I've got to know."

There was no answer.

"When I think about those things my head is just crazy."

"Cooper can tell you. Ask him."

There was no sleep for Alex that night. The next morning he could scarcely wait for his cousin to get out his Bible once more and begin to explain it to him again. But as soon as he did the questions came, spilling out of his confused, bursting heart.

"I only do bad things, Isaac," he said. "I never did anything for God. Why does God love me?"

"The Bible says He loves you. That is all I know."

75

That simple statement satisfied Isaac, but not Alex. He had to be able to understand the reasoning, to examine it critically.

Evenings the missionary continued the Bible study in the book of John. Alex listened quietly. It wasn't long until Cooper sensed that Alex was disturbed about something.

"Do you have questions that trouble you, Alex?" he asked.

Desperation was mirrored in the nervous young visitor's eyes.

"Isaac is a Christian now. How does that keep him from drinking?"

Cooper replied thoughtfully. "Christ has freed him from the power of sin. He can do the same for you, if you decide to let Him."

Alex considered what the white man said. Cooper was one of the few he could believe and trust. The missionary wasn't trying to tell him things that would make him think they were friends. He wasn't trying to get in good with him so he could cheat him out of his furs or fish, or sell him rotten whiskey for outrageous prices. When he spoke it was in truth. He was a man of honor. Even those who didn't like him had to say as much.

Yet as Alex pondered Cooper's words he could not grasp their meaning. He said Christ freed Isaac from the very desire to drink and He could do the same for him. But how? That was what troubled Alex. How could He do such a thing when Alex could do nothing to help himself.

"When we confess our sin and put our trust in Christ He saves us," the missionary continued, selecting his words with great care, "so we will go to heaven when we die. But this isn't all. He makes us over, Alex. He makes new men of us, so we're free from the old sins that hold us so tightly."

Alex was thoughtful. "And that is what it means, being born again?"

"*Ehe*," the missionary used one of the few Soulteaux words he knew. "That is what it means to be born again."

76

Two days later Isaac was once more having Bible study with his youthful cousin. Suddenly he asked a question.

"Alex, what do you do if you are lost and hungry in the woods? You haven't got a rifle and you don't have snares or anything to kill rabbits or squirrels. You are very hungry."

Alex nodded fervently. This was something he could understand. He had been lost and hungry more than once.

"I try to find my way," he said quickly.

"*Ehe*. And so would I," Isaac continued. "You come to a river by and by. There you find a canoe. When you get to the river you know where you are. There is one settlement upstream and one settlement downstream. Which way would you go?"

Alex spoke quickly. This was no difficult decision. With an empty belly and tired arms a man would go downstream. "I'd want to go fast, so I would go with the current."

Isaac nodded. "That is the way sinners are, Alex. They go the easy way. They don't want to go upstream. That is why so many of them don't want to become Christians. They want to go the easy way."

Alex thought about that. Here was something that made sense to him. Something he could understand. This was the reason only Isaac of all the men in the settlement had taken his stand with Christ and the missionary.

It was not easy to become the new man Cooper talked about. It was not easy to turn his back on the old way of life he found so enjoyable—at least it seemed enjoyable when he considered giving it up.

But this must be what God demanded of a man.

This being born a second time was not a thing to be undertaken lightly.

Isaac continued with his Bible study, but he had lost his lone pupil. Alex was so troubled he scarcely heard what his cousin was saying.

9

In spite of the turmoil in Alex's heart he continued to study the Bible with Isaac during the day and go over to Cooper's for a second session at night. On one such occasion the missionary handed him a tract as he was about to leave. Alex mumbled his thanks and stuffed it into his pocket.

It was not until the following day that he thought about it. He considered the words with care. They were simple and easy to understand. No more simple than Cooper's explanation, but when he held the paper in his hand he could go over the words as many times as he wished. He could read them and reread them, pondering their meaning until he was able to grasp all that they spoke about.

Isaac saw what he was doing. "Good, eh?"

Alex mumbled something and went back to the paper in his hand. By the time they went to the missionary's for Bible study he had all but memorized the tract.

That evening interest was so keen in the Bible study at Cooper's that it was early morning before they stopped asking questions and were dismissed after prayer. Alex and Isaac were the last to leave.

Finally Alex fished the tract from his pocket and held it out. "I want to do what it says here," he blurted.

The missionary pretended not to understand. "What do you mean, Alex?"

The Indian flushed slightly. Now he had to express it in words. This was more difficult. "I want to be a Christian."

Their gaze met forcibly, and Cooper's intent blue eyes seemed to bore into the depths of Alex's soul. It was all Alex could do to keep from looking away.

"Do you know what it means to be a Christian?"

The Soulteaux did not answer immediately. When he did the words were hesitant and uncertain. "Isaac and I have thought it out."

They returned to the living room and sat down. Again Cooper patiently explained God's plan for salvation, proving each statement with Bible verses to make certain all was clear in the Indian's mind.

"I understand," Alex declared when the missionary finished. "This is what I want for my life."

However, Cooper did not pray with him immediately. "I want you to be certain you really want it. You see, Alex, it is not going to be easy for you to live for Christ."

"I know."

"Some of your friends will make fun of you."

"They laugh at me now when I'm drunk," he said simply.

"They aren't going to be happy to see that you're living a different life than they are. They'll try to get you to gamble, drink and steal again, and to live the same as they are."

The younger man's eyes clouded. This was something he hadn't expected.

"But you say God will help me," he protested.

"He will help you. That I can promise you. But He'll only

help you if you'll be honest and dedicate your life completely to Him." Cooper paused. "You see, Alex, God wants all of you, or none of you. He's not interested in getting only the part of you that you want to get rid of."

Alex nodded. This he understood from what Isaac had shown him in the Bible. To be a Christian and only live for Christ part of the time, would be like a man taking a wife and only letting her live with him on Mondays and Fridays.

"But that doesn't mean God isn't interested in you," the white man explained. "Or that He doesn't want to save you. He does. If you're disgusted with the sin in your life and want to turn from it, all you have to do is to accept His salvation. He'll give you the strength you will need to overcome the power of liquor in your body, or any other sin in your life."

A new glimmering hope flashed in the Soulteaux's dark face. "I want to be a Christian," he repeated, even more firmly than before.

Cooper seemed satisfied that Alex completely understood. "If you really mean it, we can kneel and pray."

The missionary motioned to a little bench in the living room.

Alex remained motionless. "I mean it," he mumbled, "but I—I don't know how to pray. Can I pray what it says on the back of this?" he asked, the tract in hand.

"God doesn't care what words you use, Alex. He only looks into your heart."

And so they knelt. Alex stumbled through the prayer that was printed on the back of the tract.

* * *

During the days that followed Alex went with Isaac to speak to the men of the village about Christ and what He could do for them. And every night they joined the men who gathered at Cooper's for Bible study.

There were those who accepted Christ as their Saviour and Alex was thrilled about it, but he was increasingly concerned about a young Indian who used to do commercial fishing with him.

"God has been talking to me about Simeon," he said. "I think I'll go see him today."

"Baldhead?" Isaac echoed. "You won't get anywhere talking to him about Jesus."

"He drinks like I did before I let Jesus into my life."

"You see Baldhead. I'll go see somebody else."

Alex went to Simeon's makeshift cabin alone. It was smaller and dirtier than the one Alex had lived in at Red Lake, if that was possible. The table was made of three rough ten-inch planks nailed together and supported precariously by two-by-fours. An upended crate served as one chair and a stool served as the other. A mattress and a few dirty blankets in the corner were all that he had for a bed.

"Come on in, Alex," Baldhead slurred, stumbling to his feet. "Ain't seen you since you came back from Windigo."

Alex sat down on the upturned fish box.

"If you come to get a drink, you'd better go someplace else, Alex. I just finished my last bottle. Ain't got a drop of whiskey in the place. Not even any beer." He giggled. "Maybe I have to sober up, eh? A fellow can't stay drunk on water."

Alex did not answer him. What could he say to one as drunk as Simeon? How could he make him understand?

Baldhead, however, had something else in mind. He lurched to the stool and dropped heavily on it, grasping the table with both hands to keep from falling.

"I'm glad you came to see me today, Alex. You're a good friend. You're the best friend I've ever had." He thought about that momentarily. "Yeah, Alex, you're the best boss I've ever worked for. You go and buy us a bottle, eh? So we can drink together like we used to."

Alex had been expecting this. It was the way of his people. Simeon would have shared his last bottle or his last piece of meat with Alex. Now he expected Alex to do the same with him.

"I can't buy you any liquor, Baldhead."

His host's bleary, red-veined eyes clouded.

"You fish for Harmon. You've got money."

"It isn't the money, Simeon. I am a Christian now. I don't buy whiskey anymore."

Simeon's eyes widened and a sneering laugh tugged at the corners of his mouth.

"You!"

Alex fumbled with the Bible he was carrying and he felt the color rush to his cheeks. This was the first time anyone had acted this way with him since he accepted Christ as his Saviour. "God helped me to stop drinking. He can help you."

Simeon laughed. "Who wants to stop drinking? Drinking whiskey is the best fun there is." He reached for a glass on the table but couldn't guide his hand and knocked it over.

"Go talk to somebody else, Alex." His laughter was harsh and mocking. "It's no good for you to preach to me," he sneered. "It's no good for anybody to preach to Baldhead."

His chin sagged to his chest and he dozed off. He didn't even know when Alex left.

Talking to people about Jesus wasn't the way Alex had thought it would be. It was hard to put the things about God into words. It was hard to get anyone to listen. Harder than he had ever thought it would be. He planned on talking with several others that afternoon, but after the way Baldhead treated him he couldn't risk it. He scuffed over the packed snow path to the Hudson Bay store where he sat near the stove listening to the men.

Perhaps it was his disappointment over not getting to talk with Simeon that caused him to remember Theodore Tobias' dire warning from the spirits that he was going to die soon.

Now that he was a Christian the warning didn't hold the same terror for him that it had before. But it was still there, gnawing at his heart like an ugly canker. What was there in life for him now? How could he plan for anything when his life was to be over so soon? Even if he got married he would scarcely live to see a son born, let alone watch him grow into manhood and take pride in his strength and skills.

All of that would be denied him. Death was going to come soon. Too soon. Even though he no longer feared going to hell there was fear within him at the thought of dying.

Maybe there was something in the Bible that would help him. Maybe God would even give him strength for this. Alex stared sleeplessly up at the ceiling and prayed for morning to come so he could go see the missionary. As soon as breakfast was over he ran to Cooper's.

The missionary was in a small shed making a piece of furniture when Alex got there.

He was so disturbed that he did not wait until they visited for a time before blurting out his story. He told Cooper of Mathias' visit and what the witch doctor at McFarland had said.

"And now I want to know something." Alex's young voice quavered. "Can God give me strength for this?"

Cooper lay aside his tools and sat down on a workbench facing the youthful Soulteaux. For a brief instant Alex fought against an almost overwhelming impulse to turn and dash away before Cooper started to laugh at him. The white man couldn't understand about such things as witch doctors and evil spirits and the hex and Windigo. He would surely laugh at him.

But there was no laughter in Cooper's voice. "Yes, Alex," he said gently, "God will give you strength, even for this."

"To—to die?" the boy echoed. "When I am so scared of dying?"

"He will give you the strength to live."

Alex's eyes widened. At first he couldn't understand what Cooper was talking about.

"God will protect you," the missionary repeated.

"But—but Theodore said the spirits told him that I would die soon—as soon as Mathias loses his power over the spirits."

Cooper did not answer his protest with a simple statement. He went on to explain in another way. "The Bible says we are children of God when we are saved, doesn't it?"

"*Ehe.*"

"If you had a son and someone was going to do something bad to him, what would you do?"

Alex's eyes flashed. "I would chase the bad one away!"

"Would you let him hurt your son?"

"*Kawin!*" He spat out the word. "I would see this bad one could not hurt him! I would take care of my son."

Cooper spoke slowly, carefully. Alex's mind was perceptive. He liked to savor new thoughts. He liked to examine them from every side—to ponder them and their meaning.

"Would you make a better father than God?" the missionary insisted quietly.

"No!" Awe hushed his voice. "No! I would not be a better father than God! Nobody could be a better father than God!"

"That is right, Alex." He too spoke as slowly, as softly as his Indian guest. "Then you know that God will protect you and give you the courage and strength you need in this matter, Alex. You can trust Him!"

Alex considered the missionary's simple illustration. Even those who did not know Christ as Saviour often took the Bible to bed with them to keep the evil spirits away. If Christ was in the heart he would be safer yet. And that's the way it was with him now. Jesus lived within him. He would keep the evil spirits away.

Alex's smile reflected a thankful heart.

*   *   *

Alex spent the rest of the winter at Round Lake, living with Isaac's family. Although the two men continued to work with the missionary and saw an interest in the things of God begin to grow among the people, Alex was lonely. It had been months since he had seen any of his family. At last he mentioned it to Isaac.

"I think I'd like to go back to Sachigo."

"Hmmm." Isaac set his cup of tea on the table in front of him.

He knew something about loneliness himself. His own

heart groaned when he thought of his wife so far away from them in the sanatorium for so many months.

"Maybe it is good that you go back to Sachigo."

Seeing that there were more words in his cousin's mouth, Alex waited. At last Isaac continued. "How old are you, Alex?"

"Twenty."

"Twenty? Hmmm. Are your brothers doing anything about finding you a wife?"

Alex shook his head. "No," he replied, "they haven't said anything about it."

Isaac picked up his tea and drained the cup in one gulp.

"It is settled," he announced. "You and I will go to Sachigo. I'll find a wife for you."

Alex eyed him curiously. He didn't know for sure whether this was what he wanted or not. It was the old way. A Soulteaux father or brother or uncle made arrangements with the father of a suitable girl. And even if they didn't like each other, public pressure was so great that they usually had to marry.

"You know of some girl in Sachigo, Alex? Some girl you would like to have me see about?"

A shy smile lighted the boy's face. He had never gone with her, but she was slight and delicate and as beautiful as a flower.

"Yes," he said softly. "I know of one."

10

The warming April sun began to rot the hard-packed drifts of the winter snows. It was soft and spongy underfoot and brown with tiny rivulets of icy water that trickled downward on their way to the lakes and streams. The day was soon coming when they would swell to a mighty flood and the lakes would waken noisily from their frozen sleep. Leads would open with the boom of exploding dynamite and the ceaseless roar of ice jamming ice and piling high along the shores would echo and reecho through the silent forests.

The Soulteaux did not complain about the winter or the cold. They accepted both as stoically as they did every other hardship that came their way. But once the winds began to warm and the snows went down, a festive air settled over the isolated settlements. Fishermen looked to their nets and boats, and those with outboard motors began to scheme how to get them in repair. The manager of the Hudson Bay store checked over his summer merchandise and made ready to buy the spring pelts of the trappers still on their lines. Even the laughter of the children brightened. When the snows were gone the green of summer was not far behind.

Rose Mirasty was glad for the opportunity to be out in the sun, even though it meant helping her mother wrestle with the heavy moose hide her father had brought home the day before. They fleshed the big hide, stretched it carefully and put it up on posts high enough to keep the dogs from getting it. When it was dry they would tan it over a smoky wood fire. Then the work would begin. There were moccasins to make for her father, moccasins for a younger sister and a pair to send to the Pas to be sold to tourists.

She hadn't said anything to her father about the moccasins she was going to make to sell. He would only storm about them. Her mother knew and that was enough.

She hoped she would get them finished in time for the next mail. She already had the beadwork done, neat patches of moose hide covered with plastic to protect the leather from the oil of her hands, and sewed with nylon net thread. They were beautifully done. Her aunt, who was the best in the settlement, had taught her well. Once the moccasins were finished she would stitch on the beads and mail them to the store at the Pas, hoping for a quick check.

With the money she would get from the moccasins and the beautiful male mink she trapped two weeks before she would be able to go to Kenora and find work. She wouldn't have to stay in Sachigo where there was nothing to do except refuse the advances of boys whose only interest was in taking a girl off into the bush. The fire in her eyes and the angry flush in her face when they approached her made them see that she meant what she said, so they left her alone. Very much alone.

She worked at home with her mother and longed for the day when she could go somewhere else to get a job and have money to buy pretty things.

Her mother, wizened and bent with childbearing, squinted at the sun. "Get some water from the lake, Rose," she ordered. "I'll fix the fire and start the bannock."

Her mother knew she didn't like to cook or clean, so she did that part of the work while Rose carried water, cut wood for the fire, and made moccasins and mukluks.

Dutifully she got the water pails and went swinging in the direction of the Hudson Bay dock. She was as slender and graceful as a fawn, as gay and saucy as a red squirrel and as shy as a hummingbird.

Her father wasn't going to like it when she went to Kenora to work. He already had forbidden her to go, but her mother said it was all right, so she was going.

Many of the girls her age in the settlement were already married. But if her father arranged a marriage for her it would probably be with some fat old man at least twenty-five years old.

As she approached the dock, the canoe carrying Isaac and Alex nosed ashore. Her eyes met Alex's briefly before she looked away. She had known Alex for as long as she could remember. He had been pointed out to her as a bad one by her father and brothers. They told her not to have anything to do with him.

* * *

Isaac and Alex separated at the dock. Alex went to his brother Pete's house, where he planned to spend the night, while Isaac made his way to the Mirasty house, almost following Rose to the door. It had been a long while since Gordy Mirasty and Isaac had seen each other and there was much for them to talk about. They gossiped about some of the people they both knew and talked about the trapping, the fishing and the scarcity of game. At last Isaac got around to the purpose of his visit.

"Do you have a daughter who isn't married, Gordy?" he asked. Isaac already knew the answer. That was why he came. But there had to be a starting place for the conversation.

88

Gordy smiled. Indeed he did have a daughter who was not married. Rose was fifteen and a delight to his heart. No father ever had a better or sweeter daughter. She was fiery, it was true, like her mother and older sisters, but he knew the gentleness in her laughing eyes, the softness of her heart.

Her nimble fingers were as skilled at setting traps and tanning moose hide as they were at fashioning moccasins and intricately beaded designs.

He paused in his thoughts.

It was true that she didn't know much about cooking or cleaning house, but that was only because her mother had never insisted that she learn to do those things. She could learn. And one day she would make some man a fine wife.

"I have a cousin who isn't married," Isaac went on.

"Is that so?" Gordy echoed.

"I think it is time he gets married."

"Hmmm." There was a brief pause. "Do I know him?"

"Alex. Alex LeLiberte."

"Hmmmm. The wild one."

"He doesn't drink anymore," Isaac assured him. "He doesn't gamble or chase around. He'll make your daughter a good husband."

Gordy considered the matter. "I've heard good things about him. They tell me he lives a good life now." He got to his feet. "I'll think about it, Isaac."

Alex's cousin arose to go. He had not expected an answer immediately. In the *nanantow onikwaniw*, the Soulteaux custom of parent-arranged marriages, it was not considered proper to act too interested at first. It would look as though there were no other chances for the daughter, that she would have to leap into this marriage or remain single.

For a long while after Isaac left, Gordy remained motionless in his chair, his gaze riveted at the floor. Rose was fifteen and getting restless. Only the week before she had come to him and announced that she was going out to find work. It would be better for her to settle down as the wife of some good man than to go to Kenora where she might get into bad trouble.

He stood suddenly, his mind made up.

When Isaac came back at the end of the week he had his answer.

"Then it's settled," Isaac said. "I'll tell Alex. You tell Rose."

Rose's father did not carry out his part of the arrangement immediately. Telling her that she was going to get married would not be as easy as talking to Isaac. For all her youth and gentleness there was a certain fire in her. And she still talked firmly of going to Kenora to get a job. She might think she had something to say about the matter.

He sighed wearily and returned to his chair. That night Gordy was sitting alone in the house when she finished the supper dishes. She came into the little living room, brushing a few strands of raven hair from the dark oval of her face.

"Rose?" he boomed.

"Yes." Their eyes met.

Never had she seemed lovelier or more unapproachable. She was more a princess than his daughter. The words he had chosen with such care faded before they reached his lips.

"Did you want something?"

With his sons, or his older daughters, or even his wife, he would have blurted out the business and have been done with it. He ruled his family the way a Soulteaux should, whether they liked it or not. But Rose was something different. He tried to bring her under proper subjection. How he tried. But one look into those clear brown eyes and his courage was as water. It had been that way since she was a toddler on his knee. She always got what she wanted, if it was possible for him to get it for her. How could he tell her she had to do something she might not want to do? It wasn't easy with a daughter like Rose.

"Do you want something?" She repeated.

He swallowed in a futile effort to stop the throbbing in the hollow of his throat.

90

"You don't want to go to Kenora," he said plaintively. "Do you?"

"Yes." Her eyes sparked. "I want to go and find work."

"It is better you stay in Sachigo. You should get married, Rose, and raise fine sons."

"I'll go to Kenora," she declared firmly.

Gordy fell silent. A fine business when a man could no longer tell his own daughter what to do. He turned on his heel and left the house.

That night he considered the matter gravely. He would have his wife tell her. He would make her get Rose in the bedroom and tell her she couldn't go to Kenora to work, she was going to be Alex LeLiberte's wife. But how could he get his wife to speak when she was probably in league with Rose on this Kenora business. There had to be some other way.

The next morning he called her older brother aside.

"I want you to talk to Rose," he said sternly. "You tell her to forget about going to Kenora. You tell her Isaac and I have decided that she and Alex are going to get married."

The young man hesitated. "Do you think Rose will like that?"

Gordy's face hardened. "She is going to marry Alex anyway. You tell her that. You tell her it won't do any good for her to refuse. She is going to be married."

"Why don't you tell her?"

The older Mirasty's face purpled. "Because I said for you to tell her. OK?"

Rose's brother went to her and repeated what their father had said.

"Hmmm," she answered.

He stared at her incredulously. "You mean you don't care?"

A smile teased the corners of her mouth. "Alex is nice, I think," she replied. "Besides, I don't think I really want to go to Kenora."

If Alex and Rose both lived in the same settlement they would have started going out together, getting acquainted under the watchful eyes of their parents or guardians. Since Alex made his home in Round Lake it was different. They would have to have a time of getting to know one another, but that could wait until nearer the time for the ceremony.

They were with each other briefly on two occasions, but shyness took over and they said little. Instead, they looked at one another and giggled. Still, Alex thought often of Rose in the days that followed. He dreamed of her sweet smile, the tenderness in her delicate olive face and the fire that laughed in her eyes.

Word of Alex's approaching marriage spread about the Round Lake settlement. It wasn't long until Earl Cooper talked with him about it. It was good for a young man to be married, he said. He was sure they had chosen a fine wife.

"But, tell me, Alex," he asked, "is she a Christian?"

Alex pursed his lips. "She goes to church. Every Sunday her whole family is in church. And she is a 'good' girl."

They both knew what he meant by the term.

"That is good too, Alex. But does she know Christ as her Saviour. That's the important thing."

Alex thought about it. "I think maybe she isn't a Christian," he replied truthfully.

Gently Cooper talked with him about what the Bible had to say about a Christian marrying an unbeliever. Alex didn't say much, but he was disturbed. At night he would sit on the side of his bed and think about it. He didn't really know her yet, but already her warm, shy smile was becoming a part of him.

But there was more than the feeling he had for her. There was the way of their people he had to consider. Isaac had talked to Gordy about the marriage. He had agreed to do it and the people of Sachigo all knew. If Alex should change his mind now it would be a bad thing for Rose.

The people would not understand about not marrying Rose because she was not a Christian. They would think she was actually a bad girl and that Alex had found it out. They would think that was the reason he did not want her for his wife. And the talk about her would spread. It would bring shame upon her.

Shame for her and a terrible loneliness for Alex. Already his arms ached to hold her.

But a Christian should follow God. What was he to do?

11

At last Alex shared his problem with Isaac.

"I think I'll get Rose to come to Round Lake," he said. "I'll lead her to Christ so I can marry her."

Isaac considered the problem. "Yes," he agreed, "that's best. We'll all pray for you."

Once Alex decided what to do he was anxious to go to Sachigo for his fiancée, but that wasn't possible immediately. There was the matter of money. He didn't have much left from his fishing job for Harmon and he hadn't worked steadily since. He would have to wait until he earned some money at his new fishing job. It was only part-time work, but that was all right. Cooper was always coming to him to interpret.

Things were happening in the settlement of Round Lake. A new excitement gripped the people as increasing numbers made professions of Christ.

Alex found it easier to talk to the people about their need for Jesus than he ever thought it would be. Now and then someone who was curious opened the conversation himself.

"Alex, did you do what Isaac talks about?" a Soulteaux boy his own age asked.

He nodded.

"And it keeps you from firewater and from doing bad things?"

"Yes. The Bible says that God keeps His children from doing bad things," he answered, "if they trust Him for help."

The boy's puzzlement continued. "I don't understand."

"I don't understand either," Alex went on. "But when I don't, I go and see Cooper. He tells me."

"Hmmm."

The missionary had a good reputation among the people. He was a good man—an honest man. When he spoke nobody looked to see if his words were crooked.

"Come to his house tonight," Alex repeated.

"Maybe." Concern was mirrored on his dark face. "I'll see how I feel tonight."

That evening he was at the missionary's home, listening quietly to the Bible study. And before the week was out, he too had made his decision to walk with Christ.

Alex went back to talk with Baldhead, the one who had been drunk when he first visited him. He was sober on this occasion—sober and attentive. Alex had an opportunity to relate to him what God had done in his own life. Baldhead gave no indication that he was impressed, but a short time later he went to Isaac's to see his friend.

"Everyplace I go I hear people talking about it, Alex," he said, "but I don't understand very well. How do I get to heaven?"

Alex thought of trying to help him by finding the verses in the Bible, but just thinking about it frightened him. Maybe he would forget something, or fail to make it plain to Baldhead and he wouldn't understand how to become a Christian. He

95

took him to Cooper and stood by while the missionary led him to Christ.

There were other changes at Round Lake. Men and women quit smoking and wherever Alex went he heard of little groups of people studying their Bibles and praying together. Not everyone was Christian. Not even half the villagers named Christ as Saviour. But it seemed that every home was touched.

In the fall Alex got some time off his job and went back to Sachigo for Rose. She was anxious to go with this handsome young man who was soon to be her husband, but her father was reluctant to have her leave.

"You'd better wait until you're married," he said.

"Why?"

Blood darkened his cheeks, but he did not answer her immediately.

"Why?" she persisted.

"Because you—you aren't that kind of a girl, Rose," he blurted. "To go off with a man you're not married to."

Her eyes flamed and anger whitened her brown face. "We'll go to Round Lake by plane!" she exploded. "And when I get there I'll stay with my grandmother and auntie! *What do you think?*"

"Oh." He spoke weakly. "I guess maybe it's all right then."

Rose snorted indignantly. "My own father thinks such things of me!" It was half a day before she spoke to him again.

As soon as Jonah and Zacchaeus LeLiberte heard that Alex was in Sachigo to take Rose back to Round Lake, they hurried to the Mirasty house.

"We want to talk to you, Alex," Jonah said. "Come upstairs."

"I have to hurry. The plane will leave us if we're not ready."

"You've got time to talk to us."

Curiously Alex followed them up the steep staircase to an empty bedroom on the second floor.

"What's wrong?" he asked curiously. "Has something bad happened?"

"Not yet."

96

"Alex," Jonah said seriously, "don't let them do this to you."

"Do what?"

"Marry you to Rose."

His older brothers were so disturbed they did not lower their voices. Their words drifted down to the living room where Rose was waiting, her suitcase packed.

"We know what it will be like if you marry her," Zacchaeus put in. "We're married to her sisters."

"Yeah," Jonah said. "And all the time they nag. They want this. They want that. They're never satisfied with anything."

"They won't get water. They won't tan moose hides or make moccasins. All the time they buy COD's." He gestured helplessly. "Every time the mail comes, COD's. Your pockets will be empty like ours."

"Yeah." Zacchaeus nodded for emphasis. "And talk, talk, talk—all the time talk. We don't lie to you, Alex. If you marry Rose you have the life of a sled dog."

"But—"

"Sarah Jane fights all the time," Jonah went on. "I have to go trapping or get a fishing job just to get away from her."

"Yeah." There was a short silence. "Don't take Rose to Round Lake, Alex. Don't marry her. It'll only be bad trouble for you if you do."

But Alex was not to be changed. Although he had not really come to know her yet, already there was a feeling in his heart for her.

"You'll have the same trouble Jonah and I have," Zacchaeus warned when he saw that his brother was not to be swayed. "All the time you'll get nagged by her, the same as we are by her sisters."

Rose, who was still at the bottom of the stairs listening, felt her cheeks get hot and red. She giggled nervously.

Once Rose and Alex were back at Round Lake he and Isaac studied the Bible with her every afternoon when they came in from lifting their nets. She listened well, but that was all. She did not comment or ask questions. There was little way of

97

knowing whether she understood what they were saying to her or not.

"Jesus says we have to get saved," her young husband-to-be told her repeatedly. "He says we have to put our backs to the sin in our lives."

She eyed him curiously. This matter of sin was something she had difficulty in grasping. She knew about wickedness, about stealing and drunkenness and immorality. There was plenty of it everywhere. But she didn't do those things. She had been a good girl by the standards of her church and the settlement.

There were times when Alex was talking to her that she almost wished she had lived a bad life. Then she could confess the way he wanted her to and everything would be all right. But she couldn't change the life she had lived, and she wouldn't, if she could. Alex should be glad that she wasn't one of those who had sinned. He should be pleased that she wasn't wicked enough to need saving.

At times she got a little angry with him, he kept talking to her so strong. She had been to church in Sachigo every Sunday. She had sung the hymns and read the prayers and listened to the sermons, but they didn't say anything like Isaac and Alex said to her. There were times when Alex spoke so hard she wanted to scold him for it, but she didn't dare. After all, she was going to be his wife one day.

And so she continued with the Bible lessons every afternoon, not understanding much of what she heard and too shy to question either Alex or his cousin.

Alex was discouraged by his lack of progress with her. He had been so sure when he brought her to Round Lake that she would make her decision for Christ. He and Isaac had worked. How hard they had worked. Still her mind and her heart were closed.

Rose said nothing about their marriage day, but he knew she was thinking about it. He could see the question in her eyes. Others were wondering too.

For a time he found himself getting angry with Cooper. Why had the missionary said anything? Rose was a good girl. She would make any man a fine wife. Why did he have to say that about a Christian not marrying an unbeliever. Finally he challenged the white man about it.

"But I didn't say that," Cooper protested. "God's Word says it."

"Oh." Alex fell silent. That was true, he remembered now. But if she didn't become a Christian, what could he do?

* * *

Earl and Ingebord Cooper had started a small, informal Bible school with the coming of cold weather and Alex and Isaac and a dozen others attended it. The men worked their nets in the morning and went to classes in the afternoon and evening. Alex wanted to have Rose go to school too so she could learn from the missionaries some of those things he couldn't make her understand. But she would have been the only girl there and she would never consent to that.

Alex waited and prayed and began to despair that she would ever know the joy that sang in his heart.

After Christmas, winter began in full fury. Snow covered snow until lake and muskeg merged under a vast, endless blanket of white. Only the scrub pine and poplar contrasted with the deep drifts marking the high ground.

In the middle of February Alex grew restless with concern for his relatives in McFarland. He tried to tell Rose what was in his heart but she could not understand. Even Isaac found it difficult.

"Why do you want to go to McFarland, Alex?" he asked.

"Our mother's people live there and—and they don't know about Christ."

"But there are people here who don't know Him either," Isaac retorted. To him there were no complicated questions. If a fellow wanted to talk to someone about the Lord there was the family next door or up the path. He couldn't understand this thing Alex was talking about. This feeling of the heart.

"I *have* to go," Alex explained firmly.

"Why? Who's making you?"

"I don't know. I just *have* to go. That's all."

Cooper protested mildly but did not argue with Alex when he saw the young Indian was set on the trip.

"We'll be praying for you."

"*Ehe.*"

Alex said good-bye to Rose, took his rifle and pulled a small toboggan with some grub, his bedroll and a piece of canvas for a shelter. It was almost a hundred miles to McFarland. There were no roads. Only a narrow path led from lake to river and across the frozen muskeg to another lake. Alex was three days on the trail.

Theodore Tobias was out on his trapline when Alex arrived.

"He's been telling us bad things about you, Alex," one of the old men said, concern edging his voice. "He says bad things are going to happen to you."

The young Soulteaux winced but managed a thin smile.

"Nothing bad will happen to me."

"He has felt bad since the shaking teepee," the old man went on. "He says you won't be around long."

"But that's over now." Alex had to force out the words.

The old one looked about and lowered his voice to a coarse whisper. "I know about Mathias and what he's doing for you. And so does Theodore. He is a good one, that Mathias. But he is not as good as a witch doctor. His power will wear out after awhile. Then—" He gestured expressively.

Alex felt the strength drain from his legs and his shoulders shook convulsively.

That night Theodore came back. He was wizened and twisted, a weather-beaten old man with a face as lined and seamed as the bark of a gnarled jack pine. His beady, emotionless eyes fastened coldly on Alex.

"It does you no good to see me," he rasped. "I told Mathias there is nothing I can do. The spirits that are after you won't listen to me or anything."

100

"I didn't come about that," Alex replied quietly.

A question lighted the old man's eyes. "Is that so?" he asked. "And why did you come?"

Alex gulped. The time had come. He had to say it.

"I—I came to tell you what Jesus has done for me!"

There! It was out! He had said it! But there was no joy in the speaking. His heart raced wildly and his breath was pinched and burning to his lungs.

The old one gasped. "You came here to talk to us about leaving the old ways?" he demanded angrily.

For a brief instant Alex stared at Theodore. He knew that his face was white and beaded with sweat.

"I came to—to tell you about Jesus who can make you go to heaven."

Theodore stared at him, hatred twisting his face.

"That is the white man's religion!" he snarled. "The white man's religion is for the white man. The Indian's religion for the Indian."

Alex stared at him helplessly.

12

Old Theodore's baleful gaze did not leave the frightened young Soulteaux's face.

"You know who it was who said you would die soon, Alex?" he croaked. The quavering voice was hollow and far away, as though it came from some distant tomb.

Alex licked his lips and with effort shook his head.

"Windigo!" The word was a hiss. "The evil one himself! That's why I have no control when he tells me what will happen to you. That is why Mathias' witch power is going to wear out soon." He leaned forward until his nose was in Alex's face. "That is why Windigo is after you, Alex! He knows you follow the white man's way! He knows you have come to try to change the Indian from his religion. That is why he is going to get you, Alex! That is why he is going to *kill* you!"

By this time the boy was trembling violently.

"You're an Indian, Alex!" Theodore continued. "Why do you want to leave the Indian way? Why do you want to follow the white man's religion?"

Alex struggled to form the words in his mind.

"Windigo has put a big curse on you! *Nobody will ever be able to take it off!*"

The others in the settlement stood about them in awed silence. Never had they seen the wizened old witch doctor so distraught—so angry.

"Go!" Theodore ordered, thrusting out his arm in a sudden gesture. "Go! Go before Windigo strikes you down where you stand!"

The women gasped and looked away.

For the space of a minute Alex remained motionless. He had braced himself against Theodore's dire prediction of what was to happen to him, and for strength had repeated Cooper's admonition that God was stronger than the spirits of evil. But he was not prepared for such a burst of hatred, or for the pronouncement that Windigo himself was his adversary.

He was battling against Windigo. Satan! It was enough to water down his courage and make him turn and flee. He looked about the ragged circle at the solemn, unsmiling faces, at the eyes so empty and devoid of hope. Eyes that had never known what it was to close in peace and complete freedom from fear.

He had come to bring them the good news that Jesus could free them from the power of sin; that He could give them victory over Windigo and the evil spirits of the witch doctor. Now Theodore struck fear to his own heart! He could not stand. He had to turn and flee, to get away from McFarland as fast as possible.

Why hadn't he stayed in Round Lake and continued to go to the Bible classes?

Desperately Alex prayed for strength. Time seemed to cease and for an instant or two his brown eyes refused to focus. Then slowly he began to calm. His eyes saw again. He still

103

shook and his face was the color of wood ashes, but he did not run. *He would not run!*

From somewhere deep within his twisted, arthritic body Theodore found the strength to draw himself erect. Pain glittered in his sunken old eyes and mingled with hatred.

"Go!" he rasped.

At that instant Rene Morin, the village chief, pushed forward. He was younger than Theodore by a dozen years. Younger and taller by half a head. His face was set against the witch doctor.

"No!" There was authority in his voice. "Alex is the son of our sister and has come to visit us. Even the stranger is not turned away from a Soulteaux village. We do not turn away one of our own!"

A mumbled chorus of assent went up from the villagers.

Briefly the witch doctor stood his ground. But he could not long withstand the opposition of the chief. Morin turned and took Alex by the arm.

"Come. Tonight you stay with me."

Still trembling, Alex went with the chief to his house on the rim of the little settlement.

"You stay with me, Alex," Morin repeated, "but do not talk of the white man's religion. Understand?"

He did not reply.

It was good to be at McFarland, Alex knew. And he was glad he had come. So many of the people were related to his mother. Those who weren't had known her well.

They came to the chief's house that night, sitting about the wood heater, smoking until the air was acrid and blue with smoke, and asking about his brothers and what they were doing. There was laughter in the chief's house that night. And Alex found himself enjoying these people whose blood he carried. He was sorry when they finally said good-bye and left.

When they were all gone and he went to bed on a mattress in the corner of the living room, a certain heaviness of heart took hold of him. He had come to tell them what Jesus Christ meant to his life—how He had changed him and made his life happy and meaningful. But there had been no opportunity. The chief had seen to that.

Alex was permitted to stay in the village, but Theodore had been the victor. He had put a stop to Alex's talking to the people about the Lord Jesus Christ.

The Morin family slept late the next morning. They were still in bed when Alex got up, dressed and went outside. It had turned colder during the night. Frost plumed from his nostrils each time he exhaled and the snow crunched noisily underfoot. The light wind bit at his cheeks. And from across the way the sap in a small poplar exploded like the report of a .22 shot.

Down on the lakeshore a couple of teen-age boys were sorting their traps and snares, using an overturned canoe to lay them on. Alex kicked his way through the new snow that blanketed the path and paused to watch them.

He had been there several minutes when a voice sounded behind him. "Hi, Alex."

He spun to focus on a tall, slender young man a year or so younger than himself.

"I didn't hear you come, Vetel."

Admiration gleamed in Vetel's eyes. "You stood up to Theodore!" There was awe in his voice.

He moistened his lips uneasily, but did not reply.

"How did you do it, Alex? *How did you dare?*"

Their eyes met.

"How could you stand up against Theodore and—and Windigo?"

"Jesus is stronger than Windigo," he said simply.

Vetel weighed the words with care.

"This Jesus—" he echoed, "what kind of spirit is He?"

Before Alex could answer a small boy came running up to them. "Theodore says you should come quick!" he panted.

At the mention of the witch doctor Vetel's cheeks blanched. "Me?"

105

"Him." He jerked his head in Alex's direction. "He said I should find you and tell you to come and see him right away."

"Yeah." Alex turned back to his companion. "I'll see him in a while."

"You go see him now, Alex." There was fear in Vetel's young voice. "We will talk some other time."

Alex nodded. "We will talk another time."

He inquired the direction to the witch doctor's cabin and shuffled slowly up the path. Fear closed its icy fingers about his very being. He didn't want to face the canny old witch doctor, especially alone. Yet he dared not refuse.

The little cabin looked unoccupied except for the thin, curling wisp of smoke from the rusted pipe that protruded above the roof. The moss that was supposed to chink the cracks between the logs had dried and was falling out, and one corner of the step had rotted away.

Some of the cabins in McFarland had outhouses, but not this one. There were yellowed patches of snow around the front of the cabin, revealing the old couple's habit of shuffling only a few feet outside their door to relieve themselves. That was in the daytime when the weather was nice. Inside near the bed there was an uncovered pail that they used at night or when it was stormy and cold.

The stench pinched at Alex's nostrils as Theodore flung open the door and invited him in.

"I want to talk to you!" the old man rasped.

"Yeah."

Alex stepped inside and closed the door behind him.

Earlier in the morning Theodore had built up a fire, but wood was scarce for those as arthritic and crippled with age as he and his wife. The stove was almost out and it was getting colder in the cabin.

The frigid wind whistled off the icebound lake and through the cracks between the logs. Ice skimmed their water pail and a pail of frozen entrails in one corner. The grub box, still

106

opened, sat beneath a frost-rimmed window in which half the glass was replaced with cardboard.

At first Alex did not see Theodore's wife. She was hunched on an upturned fish box in the corner nearest the stove. Shadows hid her seamed old face even as the tattered blanket shrouded her frail shoulders.

He spoke to her, but she only grunted in return.

Theodore motioned Alex to sit down on the cabin's only chair, a rickety piece of furniture with the back long since broken off and the legs held in place with strands of fishnet thread.

Alex looked up at the old witch doctor and then away uneasily. For an instant Theodore glared at him, eyes flashing.

"I wish you would try to understand me," he blurted hotly. With that he reached behind him. When he pulled his hand back, his twisted fingers clutched an old stone peace pipe that could have belonged to his father's father or someone before him. "I could tell you a lot of things. This is the Indian religion."

Defiantly he waved the pipe before Alex's eyes. "We don't bother the white man's village. We don't want the white man to bother our village."

Alex made no comment, but he knew well what the old man was talking about. Although he had been raised in the Anglican church as a boy he knew the old ways of his people.

He knew how the boys went into the bush alone when they were eleven or twelve years old and stayed for ten days. He knew that was when they dreamed and got acquainted with the animals, and when the evil spirits would come to them. That was when sexual maturity came. He knew that the old ones believed a boy wouldn't be any good unless he followed such a ritual. That he couldn't father sons, or even daughters, unless he spent his days in the bush in accordance with their custom.

The wrinkled old witch doctor was staring at him.

"You're an Indian!" he lashed bitterly. "Why do you want

107

to leave the Indian way? Why do you want to follow the white man's religion?"

Alex answered him quietly. "Because it is the truth." There was a short silence before he went on, "Because the Bible tells us that Jesus Christ rose again from the grave after He was crucified, so we might be saved."

He continued to talk from the sixteenth chapter of Mark, describing in detail how Jesus rose again and how surprised and frightened the women and disciples were. With that Alex turned to the Old Testament and read about the children of Israel and how God led them into captivity because they insisted on following after other gods like the ones the old Indian and his wife followed.

Theodore's sharp features purpled with rage. His crippled body stiffened. Bony hands clenched the side of his fish-box chair until his knuckles showed white. And his thin chest heaved. At last he jammed his peace pipe into his mouth defiantly.

"This is the way I have lived," he rasped. "This is the way I will die! With my peace pipe in my mouth!"

He started to chant in an off-key montone.

"I'll hold my village!" His breath came out with a rush. "I'll still be holding it when I die. I'll be like this when I die!"

He puffed on his pipe.

* * *

That night Alex shifted restlessly on the thin mattress pad in the far corner of the unheated room, trying to ignore the cold that seeped through his worn blankets. For a time he was more awake than asleep. An odd uneasiness crept over him. He had the strange feeling that someone else in the room was awake. But more than that! Whoever was there was staring fervidly down at him.

"Vetel?" His voice croaked.

No answer.

Alex's pulse throbbed in the hollow of his throat and the

palms of his hands moistened. Speculatively he opened an eye and shifted position.

A spasm jerked his lean body!

Something or somebody was standing beside the mattress. This much he was aware of. His eyes picked out the great, shapeless form that towered over him in the darkness.

At first all he knew was that there was something there. Then his eyes focused in the dim half-light of midnight. He could make out a few awesome details of this being that stood beside him. He was tall and brawny, that one, in unbeaded mukluks and dark clothes. Those things Alex noted numbly.

Then his attention was drawn to the being's hands. He stared at them, gasping. The fingers were long and bony and bent slightly, as though they had become cramped grasping an ax handle.

But the nails. The nails! They were long and curved and needle-sharp, shaped like the mighty talons of an eagle. They could rip open a man's belly or close about his throat and slash the life out of him.

A tremor seized Alex. He shook so violently it was a moment or two before his eyes would focus on the bizarre apparition by his side.

At last he was able to force his attention upward. The creature's head was that of a man. But his face! Those were not the features of any living being. The nose was a great hooked beak and the eyes, round and shining in the darkness, were those of some huge, evil owl! The hair was black and coarse, but close-cropped and encircling his face like the feathers of an owl.

Alex shook violently!

Theodore had been right! Windigo himself was his adversary! He came to let him know that he was the one who was going to destroy him!

In one swift motion Alex jerked the covers over his head and began to pray.

God, protect me! he cried. *Keep me safe from Windigo! Don't let him hurt me!*

Time passed. At last he gained courage enough to pull back the covers and open his eyes.

The dread figure was gone.

He did not sleep anymore that night.

The next morning at the breakfast table he told Morin what had happened.

The chief's cheeks went ashen. "Are you leaving now?" he asked curiously. "Will you go back to Round Lake?"

Alex had to force the words past his bloodless lips. "I can't leave now," he replied miserably. "I've got to stay and tell the people about Jesus."

Morin considered that briefly, his dark face growing even more serious. "Windigo isn't going to like it."

Alex moistened his lips with the tip of his tongue. It was not easy to speak against Windigo, let alone stand up against him. Everyone in McFarland trembled before the name of the evil one. Alex wiped his face with his slender brown hand. Morin was watching him. Watching and waiting for him to speak.

"Windigo isn't going to like it," the chief repeated.

Alex swallowed at the growing lump in his throat. It was not easy, especially with one as important as Morin, but he had to speak.

"Jesus is stronger than Windigo."

"What!" the chief gasped.

"Yes. He is stronger than all the evil spirits. He is the Son of God."

The muscles in Morin's mouth tightened. "We will see," he replied doubtfully.

Word of the evil one's appearance to Alex raced across the settlement.

"Alex is scared," one of the old men prophesied. "He'll leave now."

"Hmmm. Maybe today."

110

Only the chief had his doubts that the young Indian would be frightened away.

"He says he won't go," he repeated. "He says that Jesus is stronger than Windigo."

A murmur of doubt and apprehension rippled over the men. Stronger than Windigo? This they had never heard of. Never before had anyone dared suggest that a spirit could be stronger than Windigo. It was something for a man to ponder.

As Alex walked about the village he could feel the eyes of the people upon him. They wanted him to leave so Windigo would spare him. Yet they wanted him to stand up to the dread evil one. They wanted to know if there was anyone who was stronger than he.

Old Theodore was watching him from his filthy old cabin on the hill. This Alex knew, although the witch doctor kept out of sight.

He wanted to go. He wanted to get his toboggan and run as far from that cursed settlement as possible; to get back to Round Lake where Windigo was not so powerful. But every time he turned toward the chief's to get his things he could see the helpless, hopeless faces of the people who lived in Mc-Farland. They were not only his own people. Many of them were of his own blood. And if he ran, they would never be free of the witch doctor's power. They would never be able to throw off the old ways and know the joy of walking with Jesus.

Dear God, he prayed inwardly, *help me to have the courage to stay here.*

On the path to the lake he met Vetel again.

"Are you staying here, Alex?" he asked incredulously. "Even after Windigo appeared to you?"

"Yes."

"You aren't afraid?"

Alex licked his lips. "I am afraid," he said truthfully.

"Then why do you stay?"

111

"Because Jesus is stronger than Windigo. He will take care of me."

Vetel thought about that. "This Jesus you talk about," he said at least. "Is following Him better than following the old ways?"

"Yes. It is better." Alex repeated some of the things he had learned from Cooper. Using the Bible, he explained how a man must confess his sin and put his trust in Christ for salvation. His cousin listened silently, asking no questions.

Alex stopped speaking after a time and waited. Vetel kicked in the snow with a soft-toed mukluk. It was at least a minute before he looked up.

"My ears hear," he said at last, "but my mind does not understand what you say."

There was a brief pause.

Alex was sure that his cousin was thinking seriously about Christ. Vetel would have to weigh the matter against the cost, considering the shame such action would bring to himself and his parents, and the persecution he would have to bear. It would take time for him to conclude it was worth the price. But God was speaking to his heart. He would come. That was all that mattered.

Vetel whirled abruptly and left, as though suddenly aware and embarrassed that Alex had deciphered the turmoil and confusion in his heart. Alex watched him scuffle past the yipping dogs that were tied outside an old trapper's cabin, and bend into the shack where he lived with his parents.

Alex's entire being sang. Windigo was forgotten. One of his McFarland relatives was about to make a stand for Christ.

The next day Vetel became a Christian, blurting his decision before his surprised family. His father was next. And then Morin, the chief of McFarland.

Alex's step was firm on the paths that crisscrossed the settlement, and there was new confidence in his manner. No longer did he fear Windigo or Theodore Tobias.

13

While Alex was away, Rose dutifully read the Bible he had given her. She didn't understand much of it, but she had given her word that she would read a portion every day. And so she did, sounding out the names laboriously and stumbling over the bigger words.

It was easier when Alex was with her, explaining the parts he thought she didn't understand. Not that she dared to question him when they considered the Bible together. A proper Soulteaux maiden was too shy to do such a thing with the young man she was soon to marry. But Alex seemed to know the hard parts and found other words to tell what they meant.

He had told her once that the Bible said she was bad and her temper flared. He knew well enough that she wasn't a bad girl. She didn't drink or smoke or gamble or play loose with the boys. She wasn't bad enough to be kept out of heaven.

113

Now she read for herself that God said everybody was bad. After that her heart began to ache and she no longer slept well at night.

The ministers who came to Sachigo to preach once in awhile didn't say anything about that, but there it was in the Bible— set down for everyone to read. Rose began to dread her daily Bible reading because of the way it wrenched at her heart. Yet she knew she could not stop it, even if she had not promised Alex. Something deep within compelled her to go back to the Bible again and again.

Rose hid her deep concern from the famly with whom she was staying, pretending to be unmoved when each person in the family took his turn praying at mealtime. Only Rose remained silent. The only prayers she had ever heard before were read from a prayer book.

This was different.

Finally, it was the eight-year-old girl's turn to pray. She stood and bowed her head reverently. The others remained seated, but bowed their heads and closed their eyes.

"Thank you for saving me, Jesus," she began in a halting, tremulous young voice. "Thank you for coming into my heart and making me Christian. Bless everybody at Round Lake. Make everybody Christian. Amen."

A short silence followed.

Rose's heart flamed. If a little girl like Louise was bad enough to need a Saviour, so was she. Suddenly she began to understand something of what the Bible meant when it talked about sinners—something of what Alex had been trying to tell her. There weren't any big sins and little sins. There was just sin and sinners. And she was one of them.

She cleared her throat and began to speak, stammering out her own need of God in her life.

"I want to walk with Jesus. I want to be a Christian like Louise."

* * *

When Alex got back to Round Lake from his visit to Mc-

114

Farland the first place he stopped was the Kanete home where Rose was staying. It was after dark and they had finished eating when he came in and stomped the snow off his boots. Rose looked up, blushing as their eyes met. Alex ran his fingers nervously across his face. Just seeing her quickened his pulse and brought more color to his dark cheeks.

"Hello, Rose." His voice was husky with emotion he did not understand.

Busying herself at the table she mumbled her reply.

"Are you well?" he continued, realizing as he spoke that he must have sounded very foolish.

"Yes."

Slowly Alex became aware of the fact that the conversation in the Kanete kitchen had ceased. The other members of the household were watching with amusement.

He panicked suddenly. "Do you want to go down to Isaac's with me?" he blurted.

Peter Kanete snickered and Alex glared at him.

"I don't care," she murmured, obviously as embarrassed as he.

He moved to the door and waited until she got into her parka and mukluks and boots. Not until they were out in the bitter sub-zero night did he speak again.

"It's been a long time since I've seen you, Rose." There was a tenderness in his voice that had not been there before.

She nodded. "Two weeks."

Two weeks? It seemed at least that many years.

They walked on in silence for a quarter of a mile or so.

"I have something to tell you, Alex," she began hesitantly.

"Yes?"

She swallowed uneasily and cleared her throat. He waited with patience. Silence did not bother Alex or his people. They were born to it. The woods about them were silent. The winter snows and the cold were silent. The Soulteaux spoke only if there was anything to be gained by speaking. Otherwise his lips remained closed.

"You know you talked to me about making my decision for Christ?" she began finally. "And I could not because I did not understand how I needed a Saviour—that I wasn't bad enough to need saving."

"Yes."

Her eyes focused happily upon him. "While you were gone I finally understood. Little Louise told me how happy she was to be a Christian." Rose's voice broke and she paused momentarily before continuing. "I saw that if an eight-year-old girl like her needs to confess her sins and ask Jesus to save her, so do I." She grasped Alex's arm with her small fingers before realizing how forward she was. Stepping back, she added, "I did what Louise said she did. I'm walking with Jesus now."

Since his own salvation Alex had never been happier.

The next morning he sought out Cooper triumphantly. "Rose is a Christian now. I'm marrying her."

Now that the barrier of Rose's salvation was removed Alex looked forward with eager anticipation to the day they could be married. Their first plan was to have Cooper marry them. However, he lacked the credentials for performing marriage ceremonies in the province of Ontario. So it was decided that they would go down to Kenora and be married in one of the churches there. Yes, they would go the first time Harmon's plane stopped by on the way south.

In preparation for that day Alex went down to the Hudson Bay store to see about getting a ring. Shyly he waited until only the manager was inside.

"Sure, we've got some wedding rings, Alex. Anything you want. Two dollars. Five dollars. Ten dollars."

The youthful Soulteaux looked them over. It was the first time he had paid any attention to wedding rings. He didn't quite know what to get. The two-dollar ring shined as much as the others. He held it up to the light. It was foolish to pay so much more for a ring when this one would do just as well. He held it out to the manager.

"I'll take this one."

116

"Are you sure that's the right size?"

He squinted at the ring again. It was tiny, but Rose had small, delicate fingers.

"I think maybe it will fit." He fished a crumpled bill from his pocket and fumbled for the rest of the money, two quarters and five worn dimes.

As the days passed Alex's excitement continued to grow. He and Isaac found a little plot of ground and made arrangement for it. Then they cut timbers enough to build a house. Alex had never heard that anyone ever rented a home. If a Soulteaux had money, he might buy a place, or fix up an old shack nobody was using and figure on living in it until its rightful owner came along and claimed it. The only other alternative was to build.

There weren't any abandoned cabins near the settlement and Alex had no money to buy a place. All that was left for him to do was to build. He and Isaac set to work. He was glad for something to do. It kept his mind busy.

A week or so after he bought the ring a traveling missionary by the name of Garrett came to Round Lake and attended one of the church meetings. As usual, Alex was interpreting.

During the service a bent, gray-haired Indian woman got up and gave her testimony. "I am thankful I have done enough good things so I can go to heaven," she said.

Alex eyed her questioningly. What she said wasn't right. That wasn't the way people were saved. Nobody could do enough good things to earn salvation. As he interpreted for her he changed what she said a little—just enough to make it right.

"I am glad that I have confessed my sin and put my trust in Jesus to save me," he repeated.

Nobody said anything at the meeting and he had almost forgotten about it the next morning when there was a knock at his door and Mr. Garrett came in. He wanted to go and visit the woman who gave her testimony the night before.

Reluctantly Alex got his parka and went with him. They

117

left Isaac's house where Alex still lived, and crossed the settlement clearing to a few scattered houses on the other side.

Several children, impetigo scabbing their necks and grubby brown faces, were playing along the path. Garrett spoke to them genially. Their eyes gleamed and smiles tugged at the corners of their mouths. The two boys replied quickly to his greeting and one of the girls started to speak before shyness overcame her and she looked away. It was obvious that they liked and trusted this white man who was with Alex.

A hundred yards or so beyond the children, smoke twisted skyward from the stovepipe in the bark-covered addition built at one end of a tattered tent. The tent and bark room had originally been intended as the summer quarters for some family, but had been pressed into service for the wintertime as well.

"Somebody is fixing breakfast, Alex," the missionary observed.

"Yes."

Alex glanced at his companion. He hoped they were almost there. He had to get out and tend his nets. Harmon was a friend, but that didn't mean he could get down to Kenora and back without the money for the fare. That was sure.

The elderly woman lived alone in a log shack. Alex assumed he had been asked along to interpret, but the missionary greeted her in Indian language as good and free of accent as his own.

Her wrinkled face lighted when she saw who it was.

Garrett wasted no time in formalities. "You gave a testimony last night," he began.

"Yes."

"It is nice to be good," he continued. "But the Bible tells us we can't be very good. We can't be good enough to earn salvation. We are all lost sinners."

Interest gleamed in her watery eyes. "Is that so?" she echoed. "That is something I've never heard before."

Alex squirmed. The missionary knew how to speak the Indian language. He had not embarrassed Alex by telling him

118

straight out that he had done wrong. Instead he was showing him that he had not spoken the things she said in her testimony the night before.

With great patience Garrett continued to talk to the Indian woman. He explained in simple words and illustrations how she could satisfy God and be sure she would go to heaven. Tears trickled down her cheeks as she listened.

"Do you want to become a Christian?" he asked quietly, but without insistence. "Do you want to know you are going to heaven?"

"Yes."

Later Alex thought very seriously about the incidents. If it had not been for Mr. Garrett, this woman would have died a lost sinner because he did not interpret exactly what she had said. Cooper, who did not know the Indian language well enough to have caught the difference, would never have known she was not a Christian. Silently Alex bowed his head and asked God's forgiveness.

❋   ❋   ❋

The next day he was lifting his nets when he heard the thin, penetrating hum of an incoming plane. His heart quickened. Maybe Harmon was coming. Maybe the time had come for him and Rose to go to Kenora to get married.

He lifted the rest of his nets with great haste, hurriedly prying the fish from the tough nylon mesh. When he finished with the last one he opened the throttle on his small outboard and sent his canoe knifing through the icy water. When he saw the plane he groaned aloud. It was a Cessna 180, not Harmon's Norseman.

Rose was at Isaac's when Alex got in off the lake, her brown eyes bright with excitement.

"Mr. Garrett came for you, Alex," she said. "He wants to see you right away."

Alex started for the door. "I'll go see him."

But he scarcely got off the porch when the missionary came puffing up to him, his cheeks flushed.

"An Anglican minister came in on the plane, Alex. He says he'll marry you and Rose while he's here, if you hurry."

Alex stared at him numbly.

"But—" He had given up the thought of getting married at Round Lake. Their plans had been to go down to Kenora for that purpose.

He turned to Rose. "What do you think?" he asked her. "Do you want to get married now?"

She smiled shyly.

"I—I guess so."

She rushed back to the Kanete home to change into the dress she was going to be married in. Alex dashed to his room and put on his best clothes.

The church was filled with people and the music had already started when he approached the narrow log building. He paused, searching his pockets. As he did so the color left his face and sweat moistened his dark forehead.

"What happened, Alex?" one of the men who was standing outside the church asked him.

He went through his pockets again with growing panic, but he did not reply.

"I know I had it when I left home," he mumbled to himself.

His friends noticed his consternation.

"I think he's going to change his mind, George. Maybe we'll have to chase him out in the bush and catch him and bring him back to the church the way we did Joseph Loon when he and Margaret got married."

Alex was dimly aware that somebody was talking, but that was all. With trembling fingers he felt his shirt pocket. It too was empty.

"Maybe I left it at Isaac's," he mumbled. "I'll go and see."

It was only two or three hundred yards from the church to the Roy cabin, but he was breathing heavily when he got there. He flung open the front door and dashed for the room he shared with Isaac's two older sons.

There was no furniture in the bedroom, save for a couple

of mattresses in opposite corners. His clothes were in a battered suitcase near the place where he slept and his parka was hung on a nail above his bed. There was no place in the room where the ring could be hiding.

Nevertheless he searched the little cubicle hurriedly.

At that moment a small boy burst in without knocking.

"Alex!" he cried. "Alex! Mr. Garrett wants you. He says for you to hurry, Alex. He says the pilot is going to leave with the preacher if you don't come right away."

"I'm coming!"

Still looking through his pockets, Alex ran back to the church. Mr. Garrett turned as he dashed through the door and motioned for him to hurry.

Mechanically Alex moved down the aisle. He had no wedding ring, that was sure. He didn't know much about weddings. He didn't even know if they would let him and Rose get married without a ring.

Sweat pearled his handsome young face and fear caused his shoulders to twitch convulsively.

Rose was sitting on the front pew, her back straight as a young poplar. She was scared too. As scared as he was. He could tell by the quick, nervous way she turned her head. What was she going to say when she learned that he had lost the ring?

On the end of one of the benches near the front sat an old woman who was wearing two weddings rings. Alex's gaze was drawn irresistibly to her finger. There they were, as plain as could be. Two rings!

He stopped beside her.

"Will you take off your ring and loan it to me?" he whispered.

She looked up questioningly, but did not answer him.

"Can I borrow your ring?" he repeated, pointing to the wide yellow band on her finger.

Perplexed, she took it off and put it in her pocket.

"No," he said, "can I borrow it?"

121

A minute later Alex and Rose were married with the borrowed ring.

When he went back to his room to change clothes later, there in the middle of the floor was the ring he had bought. He saw it the instant he opened the door.

14

Summer exploded on the isolated Indian settlement in a gay profusion of green. Dancing blue water flowed beneath clear, cloudless skies. With the warmth of July and August, fishing fell off and the men lazed luxuriously about the Hudson Bay dock or in the shade of the long icehouse.

But summer was only a pause, a warm whisper, and the cold began to descend once more from out of the north. Clouds darkened the skies and prevailing winds began to build, kicking furrows in the lake and moaning prophetically of the ice and winter storms to come.

There were a few gentle, sunny days in the fall after the frost painted the hardwood trees in brilliant, lavish hues. Days mounted individually, like precious stones, to be remembered and cherished during the long frozen winter.

Then they were gone. The leaves grew brittle and dark with freezing. In due time they fell and when the snows returned, the poplar forests were naked again, their grotesque fingers standing starkly against the slate of the winter skies.

* * *

Just seventeen, Rose LeLiberte was swollen with child. Her moccasined feet ached as she moved clumsily about the chilled cabin. Dull, nagging pains knifed up her back every time she stretched or stooped. The pain had come almost with the realization that she was carrying Alex's child. At times she was able to forget it, but only for a moment. Then she would move again and it would come piercing back.

A pair of half-finished mukluks lay on the floor near one of their two old chairs. They had lain untouched for the past three weeks although she would make a few dollars when she got them finished. That sort of work could be put aside, but there was always porridge or bannock to make or macaroni to boil. So she dragged herself wearily about their one-room cabin, doing those things that had to be done and ignoring her discomfort. It had been months since she felt her normal self— since she slept an entire night or did her housework without effort.

Usually her cabin was as clean as any in the village. When she and Alex were first married she took pride in having her house spotless, but that seemed years ago. During the last weeks she lost interest in doing anything. Unswept dirt littered the floor. The grub box was always out and food was never put away. There were always dishes that needed washing. It was hard for Rose even to find energy each day to read the Bible and pray.

She did not complain. That was not her nature, yet a certain listlessness dulled the fire in her eyes and she seemed not to care what she did, or when she did it. It seemed that she would never deliver this child of theirs—that she would have to go on, ponderous and uncomfortable, for the rest of her days.

Standing at the window she looked out at the children playing happily in the snow. A great bitterness swept over her. What would it be like to be able to run again?

While Ingebord Cooper was not a registered nurse, her experience on the mission field in Africa as well as in Ontario had taught her a certain amount of medicine. She had to pry to get any information from the shy young Indian woman, but what she learned disturbed her. She called Alex in several times and talked with him about it.

"You've got to see that she gets to a hospital to have this baby," she insisted. "She's going to have to have medical help."

Alex nodded. But though he heard her voice, he didn't actually understand what she was saying. Babies were born in Sachigo with the help of a midwife and the mothers didn't seem to have any trouble. At least no one made much of a fuss about it. He could not see that it made a great deal of difference if she went to a hospital or not.

Besides, he didn't like the idea of having Rose leave him, even for a little while. There was a lonesomeness in his heart when they were away from each other, even for a few days.

"I'm going to radio the government doctor and make arrangements," the missionary's wife said.

"I'll talk to Rose about it," Alex replied.

Actually, he meant that he and Rose would talk about it briefly and that would be the end of the matter. He didn't want her to go away so their baby could be born in the hospital. He didn't want her to go away for any reason.

But Ingebord was as insistent as Alex was reluctant. She radioed the government doctor, made arrangements for Rose to go in, and reserved space for her on the next plane. Finally, he agreed. Rose went to Sioux Lookout to the government hospital to have their first baby.

Alex got two messages from the hospital. The first told him that his son was born. He was so happy he thought his heart would burst because of it.

He had a son! A son to teach the ways of the lakes and the bush country. A son to show how to trap and set nets in the

125

best places for whitefish and pickerel and lake trout. A son to train how to shoot straight, to stalk a moose and to find his way through the forest. A son to bring to Christ.

For a time after Alex got the message about the birth of their baby he sat up in bed, wondering that anyone else in the entire village could be asleep on such a memorable night.

He had a son! For a week or more he revelled in the thought of it.

Then the world collapsed about him.

Ingebord saw there was something wrong the instant Alex appeared at their door. Crossing the room, he sat down on a straight-backed chair in the corner. For a brief instant she studied his sallow, intent young face.

"Earl will be back in a little while," she said. "He just went down to the Bay to get some flour. I thought he'd be here by this time."

Alex twisted uneasily in the chair. She saw that he was holding a folded piece of paper in his trembling hand.

"Can I help you, Alex?" Her voice was tender and gentle.

He looked up mutely. His lips parted as though to speak. Then he checked himself and thrust the paper into her hand. She read it slowly.

"Oh, Alex." It was all she could do to speak. "I'm so sorry."

He blinked the tears away. An Indian man did not cry in front of a woman—even a white woman. He steeled himself against it.

"This—this operation on Rose," he said. "What does that mean they'll do?"

She read the message again, not because she had not grasped its meaning, but to give her time to order the words to explain to him what the message meant.

"I don't know for sure," she replied thoughtfully. "The message says they have found something on one of her lungs. I think they want to operate to remove it."

"TB?" he asked.

126

The lung disease was a dreaded thing among their people. Just thinking about it drove fear to the very roots of his being.

"They don't operate on TB, Alex," she explained. "At least that isn't the usual treatment."

Alex was still sitting in the same chair, shock glazing his brown eyes, when the missionary came back from the store.

"Why does God do this to us?" he demanded of the missionary. "I serve Him. Rose serves Him."

Cooper reached for his Bible and read the distraught young husband the story of the man who was born blind.

"Jesus said the blindness didn't come because of the man's sin or the parents' sin," he explained. "It happened so it could be used to glorify God."

The muscles about the Indian's taut mouth relaxed slightly. "How can this glorify God?" he asked. "I need Rose so much!"

"I don't know," Cooper spoke frankly. "But if you and I had been alive and had seen the blind man, I don't think we would have realized that could have glorified God either. But it did."

For a long while Alex was silent. The missionary sat quietly, waiting until he was ready to speak again.

"They are going to take her to Brighton to operate on her," Alex went on at last.

The missionary nodded. "Is there anything Ingebord and I can do?"

Alex nodded. "I want to go." His voice was so soft it was all they could do to understand him.

"Do you have enough money to make the trip, Alex?"

"Some." He held out a small roll of soiled bills. "You count. See if there is enough for me to pay my way."

The missionary counted the money carefully. "You've probably got enough here to pay your way to Brighton," he explained, "but I'm sure there isn't enough to buy a return ticket too."

Alex was satisfied. "I'll go. Indian Affairs will loan me the money to get back."

Cooper nodded. Alex wasn't the only Indian who planned a trip without the money to complete it. They all knew that if they got away from home, the department would see that they got a ticket back, whether they were able to repay the money or not.

*　*　*

The authorities kept the baby at the Sioux Lookout Hospital and transferred Rose to the Brighton Sanatorium. They kept her there for several weeks, giving her tests and building her up physically before performing the operation.

Alex was in the hall outside her door when they wheeled her into the operating room, and was still standing there when the doctor came out two and a half or three hours later.

"It was only a cyst, Alex," he explained. Even his voice was reassuring. "We had to take out a little piece of the lung, but she'll be all right."

Alex didn't quite understand what the austere individual before him meant by a "cyst" or "taking out a piece of the lung." They both sounded bad enough to him. But he understood about Rose being all right. Tears of relief trickled down his dark cheeks and a prayer of thankfulness went up from his heart.

*　*　*

It was the last of June before Rose was strong enough to take care of him. Even then Ingebord felt she should have help and urged the girl to ask her mother to come and stay with her for awhile.

It was not until Rose got home from the hospital that she became aware of the fact that Alex was now spending a lot of time interpreting for Cooper and talking to people about Jesus.

"How will you make money for clothes?" she asked. "For food?"

The hurt came to his eyes and he did not answer her directly. "Don't you want me to serve God?" he asked.

She thought about how she had been before she made her

128

decision to follow Jesus. She thought of the joy that had come to her life, the help when she was alone in the sanatorium. The gospel was hidden to those who were lost. Somebody had to talk to the people, to explain to them what they could do to follow Christ and how much He could help them. If Alex didn't help the Coopers at Round Lake, who would? Would the people *ever* have an opportunity to hear?

"You serve God, Alex," she told him, her olive face shining. "We'll do OK."

His smile was quick and responsive. "I can work the nets. I'll catch plenty of fish. We'll do all right."

Rose's mother, who had been listening in silence, snorted her disgust and rattled the pans on the table. She did not speak up, but whenever she had to look at Alex she glared at him. At mealtime she slammed the bannock on the rough board table in front of Alex, her brown eyes smoking.

"Eat!" she ordered. "You have a wife and baby to take care of."

Alex avoided looking at her. As soon as they finished eating he hurried out of the house.

His optimistic prediction about the fishing was true during the first few weeks after Rose got home from Brighton. It seemed that he always had whitefish and pickerel in his nets, whether anyone else caught anything or not. It gave him good credit at the fisheries store.

Every now and then someone gave him a little extra money, which helped make the way easier. Even Rose's mother quit complaining, although she was still making dire predictions about the future.

Then the fishing began to dwindle.

Alex wasn't able to work his nets regularly, for one thing. Someone was always coming to get him to interpret. Or someone would want to go to an outlying district to visit. That cut in on his catch considerably. And when he did get out to lift his nets, the catch was small.

Alex and Rose had never had money enough ahead to lay

in a sizable supply of meal and flour and tea. And if they had, they would not have done so. It was not the way of the Soulteaux. Few among them ever considered laying aside anything for the future. They smoked fish and smoked a little moose meat, but the visitors who dropped by were rewarded so generously the supply soon dwindled. And no one seemed to be concerned about it. After all, nobody laid aside anything for the future. Now Alex and Rose had almost nothing. Often all she had to fix was smoked fish or some dried moose or bear they had been given.

When Alex had a few fish to sell he took most of his money in groceries from Harmon's store; a little flour, some shortening, and dried milk or tea. When he had no money he went to the Hudson Bay store and put it on their bill.

Several times the manager talked with him about the size of the account he had there.

"You're getting close to your credit limit, Alex," he said. "I wish you'd make arrangements to pay something on it. I don't want to have to cut you off."

"We get our allotment soon," he replied, counting the days on his fingers. "I'll pay then."

But when the government checks arrived there was a COD of Rose's that he hadn't expected, and some other things that had to be paid. He was only able to make a token payment on their growing bill.

He felt the cold disapproval of his mother-in-law, but she did not give voice to her feelings, except to urge them to let her take the baby home with her.

"You need rest, Rose," she said. "And Baby Ernest needs milk and good food."

Significantly she glanced at Alex. He looked away and pretended not to hear what she was saying.

Alex had to admit that the baby had not been well. He cried more than most babies, even when he was in his cradle, and that was unusual. Indian babies seemed to get enough security from the cradleboards to keep their crying to a minimum.

130

Ernest was thin too, far thinner than he should have been for his age. It hurt Alex's heart just to look at him.

"What do you think, Alex?" Rose asked when they were alone together.

Discouragement clouded his dark eyes, but he did not answer her directly. "I think I'll quit," he retorted. "I'll go back to fishing at Red Lake."

"Mother wants to take Ernest back to Sachigo," she told him. "She thinks it would be better for me and the baby."

He glanced down at her haggard young face. The last weeks had been difficult for him, but they had been even worse for Rose. She still had not completely recovered from the double ordeal of bearing a child and having an operation. She was drained of strength and looked older than her age by a dozen years: old and tired and sharp-featured. It gave him a bad feeling inside just to see her that way.

"If you think it's best, Rose," he said. He didn't want the little one to go away, even for a few weeks. Already Ernest was a part of his life. But if it would be better for Rose, he could stand it.

Her mother left with the baby the next day. Rose and Alex were alone together. It was good for Rose to have her mother take care of the little one for a few weeks. Alex could see that. She seemed to get stronger as the days passed, and the flames in her eyes glowed brighter. But it was sorrowful to see her longing for the little one. The longing stole the spring from her step and marked her face with sadness.

Alex continued to interpret and work with the missionaries, but the joy had gone out of it. The joy was even gone from reading the Bible and praying. How could a man be happy when there was no food for his wife and baby? When there was no money, even for dried milk?

Financial conditions got no better for them. And finally the day came when the manager at the Bay shut off his credit.

"I'm sorry, Alex, but we can't let you have anything more until you get this bill paid."

131

"But I'll pay you," the young Soulteaux replied lamely. "As soon as the support comes in, I'll pay you."

"We have a policy."

Numbly Alex left the store. That had happened before. It had happened to everyone in the settlement at one time or another. There was no shame attached to it. On other occasions Alex had been catching fish so he could buy at Harmon's store. Now that fishing was not good, there was nothing with which to buy.

Alex fought the matter out in his mind, lying awake most of the night wrestling with it. He wanted to keep on helping the missionary. He enjoyed the interpreting and talking with people about Jesus. He liked to sit in the house with Cooper and his wife, studying the Bible or talking about the things that happened during the day. There was a feeling about serving God that gave a man joy he could get in no other way.

Yet he and Rose had to have grub to eat. They had to be able to buy clothes and pay for a COD once in awhile. God must not care whether he served Him or not, or He'd see that they had what they needed.

Alex made his decision.

He couldn't get money enough to buy what they had to have while working to serve God, so he was going to quit. He was going to find work somewhere else—where he would know that he was going to get paid. It wasn't easy deciding to leave God's work. Yet, what else could a man do?

He got up early and left the house without saying anything to Rose. Before seven o'clock he was knocking at Cooper's door.

The missionary and his wife weren't going to like his decision. He knew that already. And they would try to talk him out of it. But that wasn't going to make any difference. He was going to leave Round Lake and go back to working for a commercial fisherman. He wasn't going to have Rose and Ernest in need again.

15

While Alex went to Red Lake to get a job commercial fishing, Rose went back to Sachigo to her parents. She moved into the family home, taking her place as though she had never been away. Her younger sisters helped take care of Ernest and she assumed a portion of the responsibilities at home.

Although they asked her no questions, she told them about Alex leaving Round Lake. They accepted the news without comment, but it was clear they were pleased to know he was no longer helping the missionary.

Religion was the only thing Gordy Mirasty had against Alex. Actually he liked the slender, kindly young Soulteaux who was so good to his daughter and didn't run around or gamble or drink. He always treated his son-in-law well when he came to visit, but this religion was something different. It made Alex queer. Now, Gordy thought with considerable satisfaction, maybe Alex was coming to his senses.

It seemed good to Rose to be home once more. It seemed as though she had not been away. But every time she saw the baby in his *takinakan*, her heart was heavy with loneliness for her young husband.

It was good to be among her old friends once more, and to work with her family. She helped her mother flesh a moose hide and tan it over a small smoky fire to a rich brown softness that had the pungent smell of smoke.

Choosing the best portion of the hide she made a pair of moccasins for her father, beading an intricate design on them. Proudly he held them up for all to see. He put them on and wore them wherever he went, calling attention to them himself, if those he met failed to notice.

"Rose made these for me," he boasted. "Look at them. Not even my grandmother did beadwork so well."

Rose pretended not to notice, but her cheeks flushed with pride. That father of hers. He was always bragging about her. It made her feel foolish.

She had come back to Sachigo at the time of berry picking and most of the women and some of the men were in the bush picking berries. She helped with this as well.

"You go today," her younger sister, Cecilia, said. "I'll stay home with Ernest."

It was never any problem, getting someone to take care of the baby. Cecilia was only twelve, but she loved the little one as her own. And if she wasn't available, Emily or Susan would take over. They all did well with him. Soulteaux girls got plenty of experience taking care of babies.

Rose went over to the *takinakan* where the baby was nodding sleepily. She touched his cheek with a tender, loving finger, and then left to join the others.

Rose had almost forgotten how much fun it was to be with girls and women she knew, gossiping and laughing as she worked. Until now she wasn't aware that she missed her old friends half as much as she did.

She had entirely forgotten about the baby until she saw

Cecilia flying down the path toward them. The instant she saw her she knew something was wrong. She dropped her pail and ran to meet her sister.

"Baby, the baby's sick!" Cecilia panted, her breath coming in long, tearing gasps. "He's very sick! Father says you should come quick!"

Rose's heart stopped beating!

Something was wrong with Ernest! That was all she knew! That was all that mattered. She dashed up the narrow path, her small feet flying. Fire seared her lungs, but she was scarcely aware of it. Brush tore at her clothes and weeds scratched her dark legs.

Rose didn't even realize when she reached the settlement. Nor did she remember going by the Hudson Bay store or stumbling over a mangy dog lying in the path. She didn't know that she caught her foot on the startled animal and staggered forward, almost falling, before she was able to right herself and hurry on.

It seemed to take forever for her to reach her parents' home. Her father must have been watching from the living room window. He came to meet her, his bronze face ashen. She scarcely saw him and would have pushed by and gone inside, but he grasped her by the arm.

"Rose!" There was anguish in his hushed voice.

She struggled to free herself.

"Rose!"

"I want to see my baby!"

He put a hand on either shoulder and held her tightly.

"Rose!" His voice raised. "No!"

She stared at him. Her lips parted slightly, but she could not speak. Understanding came slowly. And as it did her strength seeped away. She would have crumpled to the ground had her father not been holding her.

"He got sick after you left," Gordy explained. "He threw up. He shook a lot!" He held out his hand and showed her with

135

gestures how the little one had trembled and jerked with convulsions.

"Alex's brothers came, but there wasn't anything they could do. There wasn't a doctor or nurse! There wasn't anybody who knew how to do anything!"

Rose felt herself freeze inside. Her baby was dead! That was all she knew. Little Ernest was gone. She would never again hear his crying or see the saucy lights in his eyes. She would never again be able to hold him in her arms.

Mechanically she allowed her father to guide her into the house and help her to a chair. She sat motionless, eyes staring at the wall across from her.

She ought to pray, she reasoned, but for the moment she lacked even the strength and the will for that. It was as though she was detached from what was going on, a strangely indifferent bystander who was less concerned than anyone else. Yet she was not a bystander. Her baby was dead!

Family and friends swarmed into the house, but she neither cried nor spoke. Numbly she thought of Alex and how he would feel when they were able to get word to him.

Her father took charge of everything.

He got lumber from the Bay and made a tiny box to serve as a coffin. It was of birch plywood that the Bay manager brought in to use for some cupboards in his house. Gordy had no wood even half as fine in his own cabin. He sanded it carefully and varnished it until it gleamed in the sun.

The next morning he went out alone and dug the small grave. Others came and offered to help, but he motioned them away.

Gordy wanted to have the funeral in the Anglican church or the Tribal Council House, but Rose insisted on having it at home. Everybody in the settlement came to the service, crowding in until they filled the house and spilled out into the yard. The Anglican lay leader spoke a few words about life and death and somebody else had the prayer.

When the short funeral was over Gordy took the little coffin

136

in his hands and carried it out to the cemetery. Rose, with the rest of the family and their friends, followed him solemnly. With great tenderness he knelt and laid it in the grave. And when everyone else had gone he filled in the dirt and shaped it lovingly into a smooth mound. Only then did he allow tears to stain his olive cheeks.

* * *

Alex held the radiogram that informed him of the death of his son. Then with a sudden, convulsive movement his fingers doubled, crumpling the paper.

"Is there anything I can do, Alex?" the RCMP repeated.

Alex stared helplessly about him. Baby Ernest was dead and Rose was alone in her grief. There was nothing the mountie could do. There was nothing anyone could do. Without answering, he turned and stumbled away. Joseph would have followed him, but the officer warned him against it with a quick glance. There were times when a man had to be alone.

The slight young Soulteaux shuffled over the wet, rocky finger of land and stopped at the water's edge on the other side. The storm seemed even worse than it had been when they were out on the lake tending their nets. The wind whipped rain into his face and drove the biting cold through his thin jacket. Waves rumbled endlessly as they crashed, one following another, against the lonely beach. But Alex was only dimly conscious of the elements. Any discomfort he had known on the lake a short time before was overwhelmed by the weight of shock and grief. There was no cold. No wind. No rain. He was numb—devoid of feeling.

It wasn't true, this radiogram. It couldn't be. Little Ernest wasn't dead. This was some cruel joke somebody was playing on him. They would soon come out and tell him that there was nothing to it.

He had such plans for this little one, this gift from God. He was going to teach Ernest the ways of their people in the bush. He was going to teach him the ways of God.

137

For some reason his mind went back to the time before the baby was born. How many times he and Rose prayed for Ernest, even then. How many times they dreamed of the many souls this son of theirs would win for Christ when he became a man. Even when Alex was at the fish camp alone, so frightened he would not step outside the cabin after the sun went down, he thought only of the baby, and Rose, and God.

This couldn't be true. It couldn't be! It— But even as he protested, the hurt welled within him. He didn't want to accept it, but it was true. That fact was written in the face of the RCMP who brought him the news. It was written in the ache that lay as a stone upon his back.

After a time the officer left. Joseph went over to the place where Alex was standing, the rain beading his dark features.

"Do you want to go now, Alex?" There was a gentleness in his companion's voice that he had never heard before.

Later in the cabin Joseph boiled water for tea and fixed something to eat.

"Hungry, Alex?"

He shook his head.

He was still sitting in the same position he had been in since they reached the rough log shack an hour before. His gnarled fingers were tightly clasped together and his gaze was fixed on the moss-chinked wall across from him.

"You've never had bannock like this before," Joseph said, trying vainly to coax a smile to his frozen face. "If you bring Rose here I'll teach her how to fix good bannock. The best you ever did eat!"

Alex wasn't hungry and didn't think he could eat at all, but he managed to choke down two or three pieces of thin, biscuit-like pastry, some macaroni and a cup of strong tea. After that he felt better.

"When did it happen?" his companion finally asked.

"Two weeks ago."

"TB?"

Alex did not answer immediately. The message from Gordy

138

did not say what illness had claimed Ernest's young life. It may have been the dread tuberculosis. It took enough lives among the Soulteaux. But there was something else that was prying in at the corners of his mind. Something he wanted desperately to ignore, to pretend wasn't a possibility. But he could not. It was there! It had to be faced!

As long as he stayed at Round Lake interpreting for the missionary, the baby lived, even though there were times when the grub box was empty. Was God speaking to him because he disobeyed? Had their little one been taken away from them because he left God's service? The very thought was enough to tear out his heart!

Pushing back from the table, Alex reached for his Bible. Carefully he wiped the dust from the cover and, squinting in the feeble kerosene light, he began to read. Alex had not taken time for Bible reading since his first few days at the fishing camp when the fear of being alone drove him to it. He had been cold and indifferent to the Word of God.

How hungry his heart was for it now! How thirstily he read.

Alex had often heard Cooper tell people who were in great trouble or sorrow of the peace that God could give. He had even talked of it himself when he was trying to comfort someone with a heavy heart. But such talk had only been words— the knowledge of his mind.

Now it was different.

He felt the strength and peace of God in a way he had never felt it before. Now he knew he would be able to speak with a true heart. People would be able to see by the way he spoke that he had felt the peace he was telling them about.

He straightened slowly.

But he would not be telling people such things anymore. When he had left Round Lake to take this fishing job, he had left that cabin of his life after tightly locking the door behind him.

For the space of a minute the thought came back to torture him. Was this the reason God had taken their little one? Was this why he and Rose had breaking hearts? Pain drove to the very depths of his being in great, surging blows.

Miserably Alex went to bed, his mind whirling with thoughts of the baby, of Rose and of his decision to leave the service of God. It was almost morning before he managed to get to sleep. And moments later, or so it seemed, Joseph wakened him by throwing wood in the heater and cursing the ugly weather that still continued. Weather they had to go out in once again to lift their nets.

That morning for the first time Alex tried to talk with Joseph about Jesus and making a commitment of his life to Him. His companion listened respectfully.

"Hmmm," he murmured when he finished.

Alex did not persist. Such was not his way, or the way of his people to force himself or his opinion upon his fishing partner. Besides, it would have accomplished nothing. He read the disinterest plainly in Joseph's eyes. It was only from sympathy that he listened at all.

Alex stopped talking and, getting into his parka, stepped out into the driving rain and wind.

During the next few days he thought only of quitting his job and going back to Sachigo to be with his young wife. But he had given his word that he would stay on the job until freeze-up. After that he and Joseph planned to trap awhile. There was still the problem of money.

When he kept busy enough he could get through the day without thinking too much about Rose and the baby he would never see again. And if he worked hard enough, he was able to sleep at night.

◦　◦　◦

Rose did not expect to hear from Alex. He was never one to write letters. Even if he had written a letter, she wasn't sure she would have gotten it. Mail delivery beyond the roads was slow and uncertain.

At night she lay on a mattress on the floor in one of the upstairs bedrooms, a sister on either side, the way they slept before she left to be married. Poor Alex. She knew how terrible he would feel when the radiogram was delivered. She knew how his heart would throb with pain, how he would long to come to her. Silently she prayed for him.

The morning after the funeral she was up before anyone else in the house was awake. She fixed porridge and tea for breakfast, and was cutting another pair of moccasins from the newly tanned moose hide. When her father came into the kitchen she was sewing the soft leather.

"Rose," he scolded, trying to take them from her, "you don't have to do anything like this. There'll be plenty of time later to make moccasins."

"I want to."

Her soft brown eyes met his. The hurt was still there, deep and impenetrable. But there was something else that Gordy didn't quite understand. A cold fire that flickered bravely. There was no quitting in Rose. She was a fighter. Although he couldn't understand her, a fierce pride for her took hold of him.

Curiously he studied her. There should be something he could say, but there was not.

Before the week was out Rose was picking berries with the rest of the women and the children. The laughter was gone from her eyes, and every now and again her face grew somber. She was more quiet than usual, but that was all. She had control of herself in a way nobody had ever thought was possible. She seemed to possess an inner strength they did not have, a reserve of courage she could draw upon.

At last her father could contain himself no longer. He asked her about it. "I know you loved little Ernest, Rose," he said. "Why aren't you weeping over him?"

"Jesus gives peace to me," she said simply. "He makes me strong in Him."

Still her father did not understand. "But you are not sad all the time. He was only my grandson and still my heart cries for him."

141

"I know I'll see little Ernest again," she repeated. "He is in heaven."

"Is that so?" he asked seriously.

That night Rose's tears stained her hard pillow. She cried quietly, muffling her sobs, so the others in the room would not hear. She missed her baby more than she could ever have dreamed possible. She missed Alex. She missed him so very much!

16

After New Year's Alex went back to Sachigo where he got a job as manager of the settlement's Hudson Bay store. Living in the large, comfortable home the Bay provided for their managers, Rose was happier than she had ever been. They were living among her own people. The cupboard was well stocked, and there was always money enough to order COD's from Simpson Sears.

To be sure, moose meat and smoked fish were still the most important items in their diet, in addition to the porridge, bannock and macaroni, but the knowledge that the store had anything they would ever want to eat was reassuring.

It wasn't long until they became aware that God was sending them another little one to take the place of Ernest. They both waited with growing excitement.

Rose had gone to the government hospital in Sioux Lookout

when Ernest was born. Alex could scarcely give thought to her leaving again, even for such a reason.

"Do you want to go out this time?" he asked her.

Her gaze came up to meet his timidly. "Not unless you think I should."

"Your mother and sisters don't go out when their babies are born."

There was relief in her smile.

"Yes, that is what I think. Mother will help—or Mary D'Annette."

He put his arm about her and drew her close. "This baby will be born at home. OK?"

When Rose's time finally came and the pains were sharp and close together, she wakened her young husband. At the first sound of her voice he sat up, fright instantly jerking him awake.

Before she could speak again her swollen young body stiffened as the pains came once more.

Her fingers sought his, tightening convulsively as the pain crescendoed. For an instant or two they held savagely. Alex stared down at her. Her teeth were clenched against the driving force in her body. Her face was sallow and moistened with sweat. He stood there, immobile until the pain began to ebb and her grip on his hand relaxed.

"I'll go get your mother, Rose," he murmured, fright choking his thin voice.

"Yes!" Her lips parted as though she was about to speak again, but the word choked off abruptly as the pain once more took hold of her supple young body.

Alex did not wait. He ran to the Mirasty cabin and came back with Rose's mother. By six in the morning Rose's sister Sarah Jane was helping and by eight, little Kathy was born. Alex, who stood silently in the corner of their bedroom during the long vigil, sighed his relief.

He expected his mother-in-law to stop what she was doing and take the tiny one in her arms, but she did not. She continued to work over Rose while Sarah Jane took care of the baby, washing her and placing her in a cardboard carton Alex had brought from the store.

At first the young father was so elated over the birth of his daughter that he did not see the concern in Mrs. Mirasty's eyes. He moved silently to her side.

"Is Rose all right?" he asked, his voice raw with emotion.

The older woman shook her head. Fear dulled her tired eyes.

Alex pulled in a long, tortured breath. His own mother had died in the same settlement the night he was born. Then his baby was taken. Was the same thing to happen to Rose as well?

Alone he moved to the other room where he knelt and began to pray.

Mrs. Mirasty turned to Sarah Jane who was standing nearby. "Get Mary D'Annette. Quick!" Concern blurred her vision and robbed her cheeks of their deep, ruddy glow, leaving her face ashen. "Tell her to hurry."

Rose's sister hurried away.

*　*　*

All the women in the settlement had known Rose's baby was to be born soon. They had been watching curiously for signs that her time had come, so they were not surprised to see Sarah Jane scurrying across the settlement in the direction of the neat D'Annette cabin. Word spread and before the midwife shuffled up to the house, half a dozen women had gathered. They stood silently on the porch or in the living room, their somber faces a striking contrast to the brilliant red or blue clothes they were wearing. Nobody talked much. They didn't visit or offer to help. Rose had all the help that could be effective. The women came only to be there, showing by their presence that they were concerned.

Mary D'Annette was the midwife who had helped most of the village women in childbearing at one time or another. She padded up the steps and into the house. Alex showed her

145

into the bedroom. Just inside the door she stopped, surveying the situation.

"The afterbirth won't come," Mrs. Mirasty explained.

What she did not have to explain was that unless it did drop, infection would spread through Rose's body and she would die.

The dark Indian woman went to work, her leathery face expressionless.

"Maybe we should get a doctor," Alex broke in. "Maybe we ought to get her to a hospital."

"There is no plane," her father retorted. "There isn't even any radio to call a doctor."

Alex left the house and went out into the warm autumn sun. He didn't speak to the women who were gathered in the yard.

The wind was only a whisper and the lake stirred lazily, a few feeble ripples distorting the mirrored surface. It was the sort of day Rose loved so very much.

It was the sort of day she chose to be outside, when she found excuse to go out in the bush that fringed the settlement. Or she smoked fish on the rack near the house while kids of their neighbors played noisily in the yard. It was the sort of day when she enjoyed helping to flesh a moose hide, stretching it on poles high enough to keep the hungry dogs from ripping it apart. Or when she joined the other women gossiping in the shade of a tree as she beaded moccasins or intricately embroidered the cloths for their new baby's *takinakan*. Although she had a beautiful Hudson Bay house to live in, the most beautiful in the entire settlement, she could not stay inside on such a morning.

Now she might never do those things again.

All through the long hours of the day the women worked in desperation over Rose. Now and then she moved painfully, but mostly she lay with her eyes closed, as though only dimly conscious of what was going on. Her breathing was labored and shallow and her brown eyes, when open, were glazed and staring.

It hurt Alex just to look at her.

146

At last, shortly after sundown that evening, her mother came into the kitchen where he was sitting numbly at the table.

"Alex." Her voice was soft.

"Yes?" The sound of her voice startled him. He jumped to his feet.

"Rose will be all right now," she murmured.

He looked into her tired eyes. At first he could not understand the full import of her statement. He licked his lips and tried to speak, but could not.

"It is true, Alex," she repeated. "Rose is going to be all right."

Mrs. Mirasty's own face was ashen gray with exhaustion. After the crisis had passed, tension and fatigue suddenly robbed her body of its strength. Her arms hung at her sides and her shoulders twitched slightly.

Later, Alex remembered those things with warmth and appreciation in his heart, but now he stared at her with unseeing eyes. Only one thing mattered to him at the moment. Rose would live! Numbly he said it over again to himself.

She would live! O God! *She would live!*

Quickly he spun on his heel to keep her from seeing the tears that stained his cheeks. There was shame for a man to allow a woman see him crying.

⚬   ⚬   ⚬

In March of the following year Craig Marshall, the mission's pilot, came to Sachigo. He had an Indian evangelist, Tom French, with him to hold services.

The people at Sachigo had given up the sun dance and the pagan religion of the Soulteaux a long while before. There wasn't even as much drinking and immorality there as in some places. But their need for Christ was just as great.

The missionaries stayed with Alex and Rose and held the first meeting in their home. The people knew and liked French and flocked to hear him. When the first service was over an old lady stood.

"What do I have to do to have love?" she asked.

147

The speaker eyed her perceptively. He knew well that most of those who lived in Sachigo felt that they were good enough to go to heaven.

"You can't have love by being good enough," he told her. "None of us can. There's only one way for us to have love. That's by having Jesus in our hearts."

Alex reached over and took Rose's small, firm hand in his own. They had the love of God. God loved them so much He saved them from sin. He loved them so much He sent little Kathy to live with them and spared Rose's life when no one thought she would live. It wasn't because they deserved it. He had left God's service and took an ordinary fishing job. Then he went to work for the Bay at Sachigo without giving thought to the work he had been called to do.

And how had they rewarded God? How had *he* rewarded God? He squirmed uncomfortably. That night there was no sleep for him. He was one of those who should be talking to the missionaries. He was one who should get right with God.

He opened his eyes and stared up into the darkness. How could he confess the sin that he had allowed to come between them and God's service? How could he place himself and Rose into His hands once more?

They were both so happy living in Sachigo and working for Hudson Bay. If he yielded his life to God once more He might take them away from their good job and nice home and friends. He might ask them to give up all that had come to mean so much to them.

The next morning he scarcely ate. Rose saw his tired-looking eyes and read his listlessness.

"Do you want some more porridge, Alex?"

He shook his head.

"Tea?"

"No, I don't want any more tea."

"Are you sick, Alex?"

Angrily he pushed back from the table. "I am not sick!"

He left for the store without finishing breakfast. At first

148

Rose thought he was angry with her. When he came back at noon, however, he took her in his arms.

"I'm so thankful God loves me," he said huskily. "And I'm so thankful He let you stay with me, and gave us little Kathy."

For the moment she drew strength from his strength. "I am thankful for you," she murmured.

That night French surprised them by asking them to give their testimonies at the meeting. Rose spoke first, hesitantly and so softly only those in the front could hear her. Then it was Alex's turn.

"I think I'll tell you how Jesus saved me," he began.

Starting with his years in the Pickle Crow area he told them how deep in sin he had drifted, how hard he had tried to live a good life and do good works, and how miserably he had failed.

"Then I confessed my sin to Jesus and asked Him to save me so I would go to heaven when I die." He went on to tell them how God helped him to give up drinking and carousing and to live a good Christian life.

The people knew that what he said was true. They remembered what he had been like before Jesus came into his life. They marvelled now at the change that had come over him.

When Alex finished with his testimony the evangelist brought a brief message. "Now, if any of you want to follow Christ, we would like to have you come up here so everybody can see you."

That was all the invitation he gave.

There was a brief stirring and a thin-faced man came forward. Another came and then another, until five men and women stood before Tom French. There were tears in the eyes of many.

Alex was glad for what had happened, but it did not remove the pain that was growing in his heart. He said nothing to Rose when the service was over and was grateful that she did not talk to him about it.

The last day's meetings were held at Alex's house. Everyone

149

in the village was there.

"People all over the north are dying without Christ," French said in his afternoon message. "They don't know how to be saved because there is no one to go and tell them."

Alex was aflame inside.

If Rose had died when Kathy was born she would have gone to heaven. That he knew. He would have seen her again, even though they were separated for a time.

If these people died, they would go to hell because no one had come to tell them that they could confess their sin and put their trust in Jesus to be saved.

They would go to hell because Alex wanted his family to have a nice home. Because he wanted to know that there would always be meal and tea and flour in the grub box when it came time to eat. They were going to hell because he wanted an easy life for himself, his wife and baby. That realization seared its way to the very depths of his soul.

That evening Tom once more gave an invitation. Again there were those who made decisions for Christ. But Alex was scarcely aware of the fact. He bowed his head, closed his eyes, and began to wrestle with God.

God, I don't know what you want Rose and me to do, he prayed silently, *but I give You my life. Show me where You want us to go. Or if You want us to stay here, show that to us. We want to help bring our people to You.*

Some time later the matter was settled. Alex was reading from the sixth chapter of Acts when he noticed the verse "It is not reason that we should leave the word of God and serve tables."

That was what he was doing by working at the Hudson Bay store. He was working for himself when God had called him to serve Him.

Alex began to think of going to Bible school in the summer. Rose was pleased at his decision. Alex could see that she too had a heart for going back into God's work, even though it would mean leaving Sachigo and her lovely home.

150

17

When the month of June came, Alex quit his job as the manager of the Hudson Bay store at Sachigo and he and Rose moved to Island Lake, Manitoba, where he enrolled in the newly organized Bible school.

The settlement was different than any he had ever been in. Houses were scattered over several islands with apparent abandon, like a handful of stones dropped carelessly on a huge flat rock. A cluster of weathered shacks and white canvas tents dotted the bald slope of one island across a narrow channel from the red-roofed Hudson Bay buildings and the nursing station. The government school and teacherage were on another island, and a mile and a half across the lake was the mission station. Here Alex and Rose lived and went to Bible school.

Alex had long known a little English and had been making good progress in the language since he first interpreted for Cooper at Round Lake. But he was glad the school was in his own language. It was hard enough getting back to studying again and having to battle through the meaning of the Bible and spiritual things, without having to fight English as well.

He began getting up at four o'clock in the morning to finish his studying. When Rose got dressed to take care of Kathy or fix porridge for breakfast, Alex would be sitting at the kitchen table, poring over his books.

"I didn't know it could be so hard, Rose," he said, discouragement strong in his voice. "I don't know if I can do it or not."

She only smiled. She had seen his papers when the instructors handed them back and knew the sort of grades he was getting. Anyone else would have boasted about them.

The Bible school had not been in session long when the missionaries began to take the students out to do visiting and to preach in homes that weren't Christian.

Alex enjoyed those sessions. Visiting was always new and different and he seemed to have a natural flair for speaking. The people enjoyed listening to him.

That particular evening, however, had been hard for him. He had left home early and had gone farther by canoe than he intended. By early evening he had traveled fifteen miles and had held half a dozen services. It wouldn't have been bad if there had been some response, some indication of interest. But there was none. The people he contacted were cold and indifferent. Others were openly antagonistic. When he finally reached the last place, he wanted to call the meeting off and go home; but fourteen people were gathered in the little cabin on the edge of the reserve.

He looked from one to another wearily. They probably weren't any more interested than anyone else he had spoken to that day.

"A little girl came to her mother one time," he said in his message, "and asked her how old a person is when he dies. Her

152

mother told her to take a piece of string to the graveyard and tie a knot in the string for every grave.

"When the little girl came back she had the string filled with knots, a big knot for a big grave and a small knot for a small grave.

" 'That's how it is,' her mother told her. 'You can die when you are big or when you are little. The main thing is that we must be ready to die. We must have Jesus in our hearts and walk with Him.' "

He didn't speak long, and when he finished the people began to file out. All except one gray-haired woman.

"I would like to see how to be saved," she told him, emotion pulsing in her throat.

Alex looked at her wearily. She probably didn't understand very well and he would have to repeat the way of salvation in order to make it clear. And he was too tired for that now. After all, he had been getting up at four every morning for a month. He was simply too tired to talk to her.

"I'll come back tomorrow and talk to you," he promised.

She did not understand.

"But I want to be saved now!"

"I know." In spite of himself, irritation crept into his voice. "It's too late now. I'll come back tomorrow and talk to you about it."

Disappointment chilled the hope in her dark brown eyes.

As soon as possible Alex excused himself and left for home. He started to take his canoe, but changed his mind. There was a shortcut across the big island that would save half an hour. He turned his canoe upside down out of the reach of the waves of any possible storm and started down the path.

It was well traveled for a mile or so, but the farther he went, the smaller it became. At the second fork he turned at right angles into the bush. A little farther he came to another fork, and then another.

His pace slowed. He had been over the trail a dozen times and knew every turn, every landmark. Suddenly, however, he

153

could remember nothing about it, except that the woods about him were unfamiliar.

Somewhere he had gone astray.

He stopped and retraced his steps, pausing now and again to listen intently. He should be close enough to the settlement to hear the dogs by this time. Still there was nothing but the soft purring of the wind in the leaves and the monotonously musical slapping of ripples against the rock-lined shore.

He was lost!

Long after midnight Alex finally found his way and stumbled wearily into their cabin.

"Rose," he explained to his young wife the next morning, "God let me get lost. He wanted to teach me how people feel when they find out they are lost. They get worried and scared like I was in the bush last night."

Alex went back to the log shack on the other side of the island as soon as he finished breakfast and led the distraught woman to Christ.

* * *

Alex and Rose had two babies by the time he started his second summer of Bible school. The session had just begun when Gilbert and Alice Lathrop came to Island Lake with their twelve-year-old son, Billy, to help with the work. Gil had a heart for the people and was as eager as Alex to do visitation. They went together often. When there was time he insisted on doing other things.

"There are going to be some new missionaries here before long, Alex. We should cut some dry firewood for them."

Alex eyed him silently. That was the way it was when there was a white man around. He was never satisfied. Build on the house. Lift the nets. Get firewood.

There was no figuring them out. They either didn't do anything at all, or they wanted it done yesterday. It didn't make any difference what a fellow did, a white man would never be satisfied.

154

Yet when Gil was ready to go out for firewood Alex went along without protesting.

They were in their canoe half the distance to the island where they were going to cut the wood when Gil turned to Alex.

"Did you fix some grub?"

"Yes."

"I don't see it."

"I fixed grub just like I said," Alex continued. "I fixed bannock, eggs and smoked fish." His eyes were laughing. "I fixed lots of good grub—only I forgot it at home."

The missionary made no reply.

A little later the wind began to bend the treetops and scuff whitecaps on the lake. The blue of the sky was being hidden by dark, rolling clouds.

Gil, who was new to the north, was fearful. "Are we going to have a storm, Alex?"

The Indian squinted at the clouds. "No rain," he observed. "Maybe some wind." The slender Soulteaux glanced at the island they were passing. "There's a fishing camp here. Maybe I'd better go ask for grub."

They went ashore near the camp, took their Bibles and made their way up the hill.

A baby cried.

One of the women who was tending the gutted jackfish on the smoke rack straightened wearily and shuffled to the place where a baby, strapped in a *takinakan* was propped against a tree. A few soft, cooing words and the sobbing became a whimper and finally stopped.

The men had already tended their nets, cleaned and iced their fish, and were sprawling in the shade. Their work was finished for another day.

They looked up as Alex and his white friend approached.

"Hello," Alex said.

Their replies were low and impersonal.

155

"Is the fishing good?" Gil asked, noting the fat whitefish that were smoking on the rack beside the jacks.

They shrugged. "Some days it's good. Some days it's not so good."

There was a brief silence.

Gil looked at Alex expectantly. The Indian moistened his lips, but did not speak.

"Looks as though we're going to have some bad wind."

"Yeah."

As was their way, they talked but little at first. As the missionary visited with them, they only murmured politely, as though they were not really interested in what he said but didn't want to hurt his feelings. After all, they did not know this white man. To be sure an Indian was with him. That was good. But he was white, and a stranger. One couldn't be sure about a person like that.

Gil was genuinely interested in them. He asked about the price of fish, shared a harmless piece of gossip he had picked up a couple of days before, and admired the new outboard one of the men had just bought. Gradually his friendliness began to draw them out. Dark faces warmed and eyes glinted merrily. They had not met this white man before, but he understood them. He did not try to make them feel he was any better than they.

At last the white missionary arose to go. Alex followed him out of the camp and down to the water's edge. When they were out of hearing Gil turned to his Indian companion.

"Why didn't you ask them for something to eat?"

Alex eyed him defensively. "You said we should go."

"But that was so you could ask them."

Alex looked nervous. "I'm too scared to ask," he admitted. "I think we'd better look for berries in the bush."

Food was scarce in the LeLiberte home all summer. There were times when they only had bannock or a little smoked fish to eat. Alex set snares for rabbits and woodchucks and went

156

hunting for birds whenever he could borrow a shotgun and scrounge up a few shells.

Winter came. The ice had long since silenced the restless water, and the snow was deep on the trails. The mercury stood near the bottom of the thermometer. Only those who had to be outside dared to brave the sub-zero cold.

Alex had gone out shortly after daylight to check his snares. A lone rabbit was all he got. And unless the cat train came in that afternoon bringing supplies for the Lathrops, he would have to share his catch with them.

He turned to Rose.

"Sometimes it's hard to keep the heart from getting discouraged when we have so little."

"Yes." She came up to the window where he was standing. "God will take care of us."

"Yes." He expelled his breath slowly. That was what he kept telling himself. God would take care of them. He would see that they had food enough for their bellies. He would see that money enough for clothes came in, and that they had all the things the babies needed.

Rose seemed to have no difficulty in looking to God for their needs. Why was it so hard for him?

Alex directed his attention to the lake. Far out on the ice he saw a small, dark figure struggling with a toboggan. A man ought to have a dog for a load like that. If he didn't get help, he reasoned, he'd have to leave part of his load. Still the Indian man did not move from his position before the window.

While he watched, a large parka-shrouded figure left the house next to his, moving out onto the lake with great, distance-eating strides. Gil Lathrop!

The missionary went out to the person on the ice, stood briefly, talking with the person who pulled the toboggan, and started back to the island, pulling the load himself. The other one stumbled uncertainly along beside him.

When they were close enough for Alex to make out the

157

identity of the one with the toboggan he straightened quickly and jerked in a quick breath.

A woman! And Gil had gone out to help her.

That was something that wasn't done among the Soulteaux. Even Christian men didn't help their wives with the tasks they deemed a woman's work.

What would the men of the settlement think of Gil when they found out about this? Alex frowned in puzzlement. He didn't understand about helping a woman, especially a stranger. But he was sure of one thing. Gil didn't much care what the men of the settlement thought about his helping her. He did what he thought was right.

He was a man of courage—a man who wasn't swayed by the opinions of anyone. Alex had to respect such a person.

18

As the weeks passed and the winter increased in intensity the bond between Alex and Gil continued to grow. They hunted and fished and worked together. When Gil had visiting to do he usually asked Alex to go along. And when Alex had calls to make he took the missionary with him. They enjoyed being together and would talk or remain silent as the mood seized them. Gil was like a Soulteaux when it came to silence. It was something that didn't bother him.

But it was when Alex was troubled that he appreciated Gil the most. The broad-shouldered missionary was understanding and easy to approach. He was one a man could talk to. He understood about COD's and government allowances that wouldn't go around, and getting cut off from charging supplies at the Hudson Bay store.

As money got tighter for Alex he went to Gil often.

"Rose and I haven't got any money," he told the missionary seriously. "I don't know what we'll do when the Bay cuts off our credit."

"We can probably let you have a few things until your check comes."

Alex hesitated. Sharing was the Soulteaux way. His people would share anything they had until it was gone, whether there was any prospect of getting more or not. But he couldn't let this one who had been such a friend of his give away what he needed for his own family. Alex knew well enough that he would not be able to repay them.

"No," he protested. "That isn't what I came for." Panic lay just beneath the surface in his voice. "What do we do when we have no food?"

Lathrop opened the wood heater and stirred the embers with a short rod.

"Let me see what I can do, Alex," he said at last. "I might be able to help you."

Alex felt better when he went home. He always felt better after talking and praying with Gil about his problems. A calm assurance came over him, the knowledge that all was going to be well.

He couldn't understand why. They still had but little in their grub box and the Bay manager was still threatening to cut off their credit. Nothing had happened to cause him to feel any better. Yet, he did.

He was still feeling contented and self-assured when Phil Cramer, a mission board member and pilot, flew to Island Lake some two weeks later. Phil stayed with the Lathrops, but he and Gil came over to see Alex shortly after supper.

"I'm going to be visiting some of the churches in the south as soon as I get back from this trip, Alex," he said.

"You are, eh?" Alex couldn't see why Cramer was telling him that. The missionaries did that sort of thing every once in a while, but he didn't know the purpose of it. It always seemed a waste of time to him.

160

"Gil and I have been talking about it, Alex. We think it would be good if you'd go along."

"Me?" Alex was surprised.

"I think the Christians who are interested in our work would like to meet you." Cramer's mild gray eyes were averted politely in the Soulteaux manner. "You could tell them about the Bible school."

Alex was a long while in answering. "I'm afraid I would get lonesome."

"It would help us raise the money we need to keep the school going the way it should." He paused significantly. "And Gil tells me your support hasn't been coming in too well. We could probably find someone else to help you in a financial way."

Interest gleamed in Alex's eyes. If it would mean more money for him and his family, if it would mean they could pay on their bill so they would have credit at the Bay, it might be worth doing.

"How long will we be gone?" he asked.

"A month or two."

A month or two! It might just as well be a year!

Alex and Rose talked it over that night after their guests had gone. He didn't want to make the trip. They would be visiting places like Saskatoon and Edmonton, speaking in white churches and staying in the homes of people he had never seen before. It all held strange terror for him—terror he couldn't quite put into words, even to Rose. But they had to have more money, and there was no other way he knew they could get it. So reluctantly he agreed to go.

Before they left he had a long talk with Rose. "Be sure to read the Bible every day and have time for prayer," he said. "And see that Kathy and Stanley learn their Bible verses."

She nodded.

He didn't have to remind her of those things, he knew. But he had to say something.

"And don't forget," he continued, "pray for me." His wide

161

eyes betrayed his fear. "It is not good that a man is away from his family," he blurted.

"We will be all right, Alex. God will take care of us."

"Yes." He thought of something else. "The support money is behind and the man at the Bay says we have to pay on the bill. When the family allowance check comes, pay him. OK?"

"Yes."

*　*　*

Alex was finding the trip south anything but enjoyable. There were too many people, too many cars and too much noise.

"Enough to break your ears," he complained mildly.

"You'll get used to it," Cramer assured him.

Glumly he shook his head.

Alex not only found the confusion and speed of southern Canada bewildering, he missed the friendly quiet of his beloved north. He missed the lakes and the trees and the simple food, the pleasant musical sound of his own language, the gay chatter of his children and Rose's quiet smile.

"No bannock, Phil?" he asked Cramer plaintively as they studied the menu in a Saskatoon cafe.

"No bannock."

"No pemmican or smoked fish or moose meat." Disappointment flecked his voice.

"You like the white man's food, don't you?"

"A man needs something that stays in his belly," he retorted.

Not only was the menu disturbing. So were the crowds! On a street corner waiting for the lights to change, the bewildered Indian looked about, his fear growing.

"Can we go home now, Phil?" he asked.

"But we've just started," the missionary told him. "We haven't been gone a week yet."

Alex fell silent. Gil Lathrop and Cramer both asked him to make the trip. It was the Lord's work, they told him, just as much as explaining to someone in the north about getting to heaven. And Alex wanted to do God's will, whatever it was.

162

But why would God do a thing like sending him into such a place? Why would God take him away from the places he knew and loved, and direct him to a place where he was miserable and afraid?

He did like giving his testimony in the services. God's people were much the same wherever they lived, or whatever the color of their skin. He could feel them warm to him as he related how God found him and saved him from a life of drunkenness and sin. And when the meetings were over many came up to shake hands with him.

To be sure, he visited but little, answering questions when he was asked, but not volunteering any information. He even enjoyed going into some of the homes, although they didn't seem quite real. Beds as soft as the down from the breast of a goose, warm rugs on the floors, and stoves that didn't gulp firewood by the cord. The women didn't have to carry water into their big, fancy homes either. It came in little pipes. One for hot water and one for cold. He had seen such things in hospitals, but he never supposed anyone had them in the places they lived.

He observed that the women didn't have to make moccasins or lift nets or flesh moose hides and tan them. And in the store there were more vegetables than anyone could eat.

"What do the women do, Phil?" he asked seriously. "How do they keep busy?"

His companion only laughed.

Rose wouldn't believe those things when he told her. Maybe she would want to come out herself so she wouldn't have to work anymore. He chuckled at the thought of it.

In spite of the things he saw, Alex was not happy on the trip. The laughter in his eyes dimmed and his smile seldom flashed anymore. More and more he sat by himself, staring off into space.

Cramer saw his loneliness and tried to tease him out of it.

"You're getting fat, Alex," he said. "You must like the white man's food."

163

"*Ehe.*" He did not smile in return. "White man's food is good to the taste and makes the stomach bulge. But it doesn't put strength in a man's legs." He sighed. "And I keep saying to myself that when I go back I'll have to eat bannock and smoked fish again."

The white man's food was beginning to please Alex's palate now that he was growing accustomed to it. But he continually reminded himself that this was not for him. One day soon he would have to leave it and go back to his family and the ways and foods of his people.

He was getting used to the traffic too, even though the cars went so fast. One day Phil and Alex were riding on the highway west of Edmonton when they came upon an accident. Two cars had collided, killing several people. As Alex saw the terrible scene, the color seeped from his face, leaving it a pasty gray.

The next day he told Cramer he could not finish the rest of the deputation trip with him.

"I am too lonesome," he said.

Cramer, who knew Alex and his people well, was aware of the fact that he could press him into staying if he wished. He also knew how deep the Indian's homesickness actually was.

"All right, Alex," he said kindly, "if you want to go home, I'll make the rest of the meetings."

❋   ❋   ❋

Alex was glad to get back home, but found it difficult to go back to their old way of living. He missed the white man's food and longed for a white man's house for his family.

"They have a bedroom for the boys, Rose," he said, "and one for the girls, with beds so soft you never want to get up."

She had been out to the hospital. She had seen a few of the white man's conveniences. And of course there were the catalogs. She could spend hours looking at them and dreaming of all the things there were to buy. Things like Alex was talking about.

"Some day we'll get a fine house," he assured her.

164

Rose's expression grew serious. "I forgot to tell you, Alex. The man at the Bay wants you to come over and see him as soon as you get home."

"Is that so?" he exclaimed curiously.

"It is something about the bill. He says we have to pay on it."

"Didn't the family allowance come?"

She eyed him shyly. "I had some COD's."

Alex frowned. Always it was the man at the Bay wanting money or Rose getting COD's. He could never catch up.

He had been thinking about the bill they owed the Hudson Bay store and the financial support that was supposed to be coming to them from Christian people who lived in those fine houses and put such fine food on their tables and drove cars so shiny it almost hurt the eyes to look at them. Financial support that was supposed to be coming in, but wasn't.

He hadn't even gotten any new support like Cramer thought he would get by going on the trip. And he was disturbed about that. The fact that he left and came home too soon didn't occur to him.

"We're supposed to get $140 a month, Rose. But we've only gotten $30 the last three months." His discouragement was great. "If we'd get what they promise us all the time, we would *never* have a bill at the Bay."

"Yeah." She spoke indifferently. Money was something she knew very little about. As long as there was food in the grub box and clothes for the children she didn't even think about money.

But not Alex. He was the one who had to face the manager at the Bay.

"It almost makes a fellow decide to quit working for the Lord and go back to fishing," he said.

After that he found it harder to carry on his work.

At the little church he took up two offerings each Sunday. One was for the Sunday school and one for the church. The people did the best they could. At least that was what they

165

said. But the offerings were pitifully small. Alex didn't realize how small until he added them up for the year.

"In the white man's church the minister gets paid out of the offerings, Rose," he complained.

"But Island Lake is not a white man's church," she replied with unanswerable logic.

"Here we do all this work and get nothing for it."

"Except to serve the Lord."

Alex was feeling so sorry for himself that even that made little impression upon him.

19

Cat trains, the freighters of the isolated north, usually welcomed the cold and snow. It was in the wintertime that they hauled supplies from the head of Lake Winnipeg along winter roads to isolated settlements across the north. This year they moved slowly between storms, or not at all.

After Christmas the thermometer plummeted. Even seasoned bush pilots left the engine shrouds on their Norsemen and 180's and stayed by the fire, venturing into the air only if an emergency demanded it. Gaunt and weak, moose and caribou stumbled through the drifts, increasingly easier quarry for the timber wolves that were beginning to pack.

The skin hung loosely on the few rabbits and squirrels Alex was able to catch in his snares. Their meat was tough and stringy. All the activity at the church left Alex little time to scrounge for other game.

As long as they had plenty of credit at the Bay, he was able to ignore the fact that their financial support from the Christians in the south had slowed and all but stopped. Yet the time came when the manager called him in and talked with him about his bill.

"Why don't you put out some nets and fish, Alex?" he asked. "They're catching good now."

"The church—" the Indian said hesitantly.

"Forget the church!" the Bay manager exploded. "You want your kids to eat, don't you?"

Dejectedly Alex turned away.

He was halfway to the door when he heard the deep-throated whine of the aged Bellanca that made the thrice-weekly run from Norway House. His spirits lifted. He rushed into the biting cold, strapped on his snowshoes and ploughed through the deep drifts to the post office on the next island.

There would be mail for him. There had to be!

Shyly he waited with the others while the Indian postmaster sorted the mail. He began to hand it out, a few pieces at a time. There were COD's to take care of. People, clutching a few tattered bills they had been squirreling away from their family allowances or fishing money, never seemed to have the right change. Each transaction seemed to take forever. Finally it was Alex's turn.

The postmaster glanced at him.

"Nothing today, Alex."

His world crumpled about him.

When he got home he called Rose into the kitchen. "We're leaving the work here at the church and Bible school," he announced. "We're quitting."

She sat down opposite him. There was no need for her to ask what was wrong. She had seen discouragement growing in his manner.

"Maybe the letters were delayed at Norway House," she told him. "They forget the mail sometimes."

His gaze met hers. What she said was true. They did forget a mailbag at Norway House occasionally. Even more likely, they hadn't been able to take all the mail in one trip and left part of it until the next time.

"Once I could understand," he said miserably. "Three times, or a month maybe. But we *never* get support money anymore."

Agitated, he began the shuffle of a man used to spending long hours every winter on snowshoes.

"We should pray about it, Alex." His wife's words cut through the silence.

Angrily he turned on her. "Pray about it?" he echoed. "We prayed already. But it's no use for us to go on, Rose. God doesn't want us to serve Him. He is saying, 'Get out, Alex. I don't need you to work for me anymore!' "

Slowly he turned to look out the window. Wind-whipped snow scudded across the lake. His own thoughts were like that, cold and confused, driven by anger and bewilderment and disappointment.

Rose folded her work-worn hands in her lap.

"You teach new Christians what the Bible says," she reminded him gently. "You help win people for Jesus."

Her quiet protests only infuriated him the more. "If God wants me to work for Him, why doesn't He send money for grub? Why doesn't He help pay the bill at the Bay so we can get good credit again?"

"Maybe He's testing us."

But Alex did not even hear her as he stomped out of the cabin to be alone in the nearly blinding whiteness.

The next mail a small support check came. Combining it with the family allowance, he was able to pay enough on their bill at the Hudson Bay store to keep the manager from cutting off their credit altogether, although he still limited what they could buy.

Then the days began to warm once more. The slanting sun cut ridges into exposed snowbanks. Little rivulets drained the melting snow. The settlement stirred and began to come alive again. There were smiles on the faces of the men as they congregated at the Bay, ordering new nets and floats for the summer fishing season that would start as soon as the ice was out.

Alex had not said much to Rose. Nor had he revealed his growing discouragement to others. Yet it was apparent to those who knew him well that something was wrong. He seldom laughed anymore, or played with the children. His once bright eyes had grown dull. Even his messages reflected his dejection. No longer did they ring with the joy of salvation.

At last the long-waited breakup came. Somewhere out on the lake a deep crack shot along the ice.

A man on shore shouted. "Breakup!"

Others heard it too. Moments later a dozen men and boys were standing on the shore, staring expectantly at the cracking ice.

There was a second explosion and grins split the faces of the watching Indians. By this time women and girls were coming outside to watch the spectacular phenomenon of spring, the ice breakup.

Alex shaded his eyes with a trembling hand. Breakup! That was what had happened to his heart—his life. It broke in little pieces like the ice.

Back in Sachigo when he and Rose got back into fellowship with God and decided to go into His service, he thought he would serve God the rest of his life. He didn't think he would ever consider going away again.

But how could a man go on when he didn't have grub for his family? How could his wife make bannock without flour, or porridge without meal?

Such thoughts plagued his mind for weeks. Finally he decided that it was no use trying to fight any longer.

Once he made up his mind he left their house and hurried next door to see Gil Lathrop. He had to tell him now, while the decision was fresh and firm in his mind; while the arguments would be convincing.

"I'm sorry, Alex," Alice Lathrop said, "but Gil took Billy to visit the Keash's while he makes some calls with Fred Keash."

Alex frowned.

"Will they be back soon?"

She shook her head. "They took sleeping bags and a tent. I think they'll spend the night."

At first Alex was going to go back home and wait until the following day, but the burning in his heart was so great he had to see Gil at once. He had to be through with the matter. Getting his canoe and outboard, the slight young Soulteaux crossed the lake to Government Island.

There was something wrong. Alex became aware of it the instant he pulled his canoe out of the water. Men were standing around the dock as they always did, but nobody talked much and there was a somber look in their eyes. He spoke to them, and they spoke in return, but there was no warmth, no friendliness in their voices. Curiously he made his way up the bank to the Hudson Bay store, and behind it to the path that led to the Keash house. It was almost a mile to the cabin where Fred and his family lived, but it only took a few minutes for him to reach it.

Grandma came to the door in response to his knock. Usually she beamed when she saw him, but today fear dampened the lights in her eyes.

"Is Fred here?" he asked.

She shook her head. "He went off someplace with the white man," she explained.

That would be Gil Lathrop.

"When will they be back?"

The wizened old lady didn't know, but Billy came up beside her.

"They'll be back before dark, Alex," he explained. "Dad and I are camping out tonight."

"I think maybe I'll wait." He went into the cabin and sat down.

Grandma hobbled over and sat down across from him, her crutch and cane close to her trembling hands. Alex tried to talk to her, but she did not respond. Instead she stared briefly

171

at him and then away, her gaze darting fearfully about the room.

"Is something wrong?" Alex asked.

Billy looked up. "The diesel generator stopped this afternoon. There's no electricity at the Bay or the government buildings."

"Yes," Grandma said in her pinched, singsong voice. "Windigo stopped it."

Windigo! Alex started. He had not thought of the evil one for several years—not since he saw him that night at McFarland. Sweat came out on his forehead.

"Windigo stopped it," she repeated. "It is the time of the full moon. And he's going to walk again tonight."

Billy eyed her curiously.

"How do you know he's going to walk, Grandma?" he asked in passable Soulteaux.

Her voice lowered as though she feared the evil spirit would hear her and punish her for speaking. "I saw the eyes of the wolf out in the bush."

"There's no wolf out there," Billy retorted skeptically. "What do you mean, you saw the eyes of the wolf?"

But she was not dissuaded.

"Windigo's there! I saw his eyes out in the bush. I know he's going to walk again tonight!" She began to rock back and forth, chanting to herself in a low monotone.

Alex felt the muscles in his throat constrict. He knew about Windigo. He knew what she was talking about and just how she felt. He rubbed his neck with trembling fingers and hoped they didn't read the fear that was gripping him.

"We have the power of Christ, Grandma," the missionary's son told her. "We don't have to be afraid."

Her sunken eyes grew wide with terror and her frail body began to tremble.

"Don't talk that way!" she warned him. "Don't talk that way!" She leaned forward. "The Windigo is mad. Tonight he

172

comes! You'd better be careful! If you go out you will die tonight!"

Alex drew in his breath sharply. This young one had indeed better be careful and mind the warning of Grandma. Sometimes the aged had a way of knowing what was going to happen. A way that he did not entirely understand. By this time the others in the room were listening to her. Fear surged through them like an electric charge.

"I'll go outside and nothing will hurt me," Billy continued. "I don't have to be afraid when I have the power of the Holy Spirit."

Alex leaned forward but did not speak.

"You could come outside and prove to yourself that the Lord is able to take care of you."

As he continued to talk to her she began to quiet. Alex could almost feel the fear go out of her. And as it left, he could feel his own courage returning.

"I will do this thing," she said at last. "I'll go out and see if the power of Christ is able to take care of me." There was a long pause. "If someone will go with me."

She turned to Alex and stared at him. He squirmed, but did not speak. It wasn't his place to go outside with her, he reasoned. He wasn't the one who was pushing for it.

Billy settled the matter. He got to his feet, wriggled into his parka and started for the door.

"I'll be back in a few minutes."

While he was gone Grandma Keash rocked back and forth in her battered old chair, muttering to herself. It wasn't long until the boy came back in.

"See, nothing happened to me," he said boyishly. "You don't need to be afraid."

She looked about, her dark face still troubled. And when she spoke there was hesitance in her voice. "I want to go out," she said. "I want to prove Windigo won't hurt me."

Her young granddaughter came over to her. "I'll go with you, Grandma."

The old lady's face lighted briefly and she struggled to her feet. Beverly took her by the arm and together they approached the door. Once in the doorway, however, their courage weakened. They stopped for a moment. Although the sun was just going down, the long twilight of summer was almost as bright as midday. But that did not seem to matter, so great was their fear of the evil one. Fearfully they both turned toward Alex and Billy.

Alex moistened his lips, but before he could speak the boy did so.

"Don't be afraid. Nothing's going to hurt you."

Beverly went outside, leading her reluctant grandmother. They moved a few steps, stopped to look back and moved forward again.

Alex prayed for them silently. It was all right for Billy to be so brave, so sure of himself. He didn't know about witch doctors and Windigo and the power of the evil one. Alex got to his feet and started for the door.

Then without warning it happened.

"I can't do it, Grandma!" the girl screamed. Leaving the frightened old woman, she turned and fled, sobbing, into the house.

Grandma leaned heavily on her cane and crutch. So great was her terror she seemed unable to move.

"Somebody come and get me," she cried. "Please! Somebody come and get me!" A low, tremoring moan escaped her lips. Fear had stolen reason. She was crying now and muttering to herself—muttering words and formless sounds of terror. "Please come help me!"

With that Alex dashed forward and took the old woman by the arm.

"There now," he said stammering. "Let me help you get turned around."

"Wi-windigo," she muttered almost incoherently. "Wi-windi-go wa-walks tonight—"

Alex was praying with every step, with every breath as he

174

guided the aged woman back to the house. She was still sobbing in near hysteria as he got her inside and seated once more.

She was still mumbling and crying softly. The other members of the household stood silently about, faces somber and
eyes dark with fear. Although no one except grandma was
crying, the tension seemed to build. Endlessly the minutes
dragged by.

The house was so hushed with fear that the sudden rattling
at the door was like the exploding of a rifle.

Breathing stopped. Heads jerked up! Eyes snapped around
to stare at the cabin door!

"Wh-wh-what was that?" Beverly demanded fearfully.

Alex glanced at grandma.

"Windigo!" she cried, horror rushing to her voice. "I knew
he was going to walk tonight. I knew he was going to walk
tonight!" She began to moan and rock back and forth once
more. "What is going to become of us? What will happen to
us all?"

Alex moistened his lips. He knew well enough that the old
one was right. She had grown up at a time when she had seen
the power of Windigo. She wasn't like these young ones or the
scoffing white boy. She knew Windigo was something to be
feared, something to be reckoned with.

"What will happen to us all?" she repeated.

"I'll see what's at the door," Billy said, getting to his feet.
"It probably isn't anything that—"

Alex half rose in his chair.

"*Don't!*" Grandma shrieked in terror. Alex gasped. That
was the first time he had ever heard her utter a single word of
English.

The rest of the family bolted for the bedroom.

"If you don't want me to open the door, I won't," Billy said.
"But I just thought I'd see what's out there."

Alex was glad he didn't open the door, but from what he
knew about Windigo that wouldn't have made any difference.

175

If the evil one wanted to get into a room, a little thing like a locked door wouldn't keep him out.

Although Alex didn't say anything, he was still trembling inside when Billy went to the door half an hour later.

"Look," he said, "It's only my dog."

Alex looked at the clock. Suddenly he felt ashamed for having been afraid of Windigo. He didn't want to see Gil Lathrop that night. He didn't want to be there when they talked about it.

"I'm going, Billy," he said, getting to his feet. "I'll see your father tomorrow when you get back."

On his way home across the lake Alex considered everything that had happened. He had met his fear of Windigo at McFarland and conquered it. Why had it come back to taunt him now? Or did it happen because he was once more turning his back on God's service?

20

Alex didn't sleep at all that night. He lay motionless on the
hard mattress beside Rose, staring up at the cracked ceiling.
He had known for weeks that the time was coming when he
would have to make the decision he was facing. Yet he had
fought against it. He didn't want to leave either Island Lake
or the Lord's service. He and Rose had been happier here
than they had ever been since their marriage—even happier
than at Sachigo when he was Hudson Bay manager and they
had everything a man and his wife could want or need.

But, what was he to do?

His children had to have bannock and macaroni for their
bellies, and clothes to wear. And a man's wife was bound to
send for COD's as long as Eatons and Simpson-Sears sent out
catalogs. There had to be money for those.

He got up before dawn, built a fire in the heater and sat

beside it, staring numbly at the floor. It wasn't his fault he was leaving Island Lake, he told himself doggedly. If anyone was to blame it was those people in the south who lived in their fine houses and drove their fine cars and didn't think that in the north a man's family might go hungry if they didn't send their support.

He decided he wouldn't even talk it over with Gil Lathrop. He'd write his letter to mission headquarters and tell them he was resigning.

When Rose and the children got up two hours later he was sitting at the kitchen table, her writing pad before him. She watched Alex curiously, but did not speak to him. She even kept the children quiet, motioning to them with her hands. She set their porridge on the other end of the table, sat down to eat breakfast with them, and then cleared away the dishes. Alex stared at the half-finished letter before him. At last he completed it, read it over to himself and addressed an envelope. Only then did he look up.

"I'm writing to headquarters, Rose," he announced half defensively. "I told them we haven't gotten any support for five months. I told them that I'm leaving the Bible school and that I can't pastor the church anymore. I'm going to get my nets and go fishing."

Rose masked her own disappointment. "Who will take over the church, Alex?"

He shrugged. "Fred Keash, maybe."

"You said he's better as an evangelist than as a pastor."

"Allan Harper then."

"And who takes over at Red Sucker if Allan comes here?"

His temper flared. "Why ask me? I don't run the mission!"

Alex got his beaded buckskin jacket and went out into the chilly spring air. He first planned to take his canoe across the lake to the post office and mail the letter himself. At the dock, however, he met a friend who lived on the other island.

"Sure, Alex," he said, "I'll mail the letter for you." He shoved it into his pocket.

"I want it to go out in this afternoon's mail."

"OK. I'll stop at the post office before I go home."

Alex watched him draw away from shore in his slender, square-sterned canoe. It was done. He had mailed his letter of resignation. It wouldn't make any difference how hard Gil tried to dissuade him, he couldn't call it back. He should have felt better about it. He had thought it all out and had come to the only decision possible. Yet a great uneasiness engulfed him.

Alex was still standing near the short dock when the storm hit. It came roaring in over the treetops without warning. In one savage blast the violent winds whipped the quiet lake to a frenzy. Swells peaked, only to have the gale blow off the tops in ugly white froth and whip spray across the surface. They crashed onto the beach with a deafening roar.

Rain was not far behind. It came down in driving torrents, soaking Alex to the skin. He whirled and made a dash for the house.

Alice Lathrop, seeing Alex's predicament, opened the door and yelled at him. At first he didn't hear her. She yelled again. He turned and came back.

"Come in a minute, Alex." She was trying to act calm and unconcerned, but in spite of her efforts fear stole the color from her cheeks and clouded her blue eyes.

"Were you down at the dock just now?" she asked as he sat down in the living room.

"*Ehe.*" He looked politely away.

"Gil and Billy aren't down there, are they?"

He shook his head.

"I was afraid they weren't. I suppose it's silly, but I've been a little concerned about them." She laughed uneasily. "Gil thought they'd be coming back about this time."

"They probably stayed when the storm hit."

"I'm sure they did." She laughed again to hide her nervousness. "But I'll feel better when I know." She paused momentarily. "I don't like to ask you this, Alex, but when the storm is over would you mind taking me to Government Island so I can be sure they're all right?"

"*Ehe*. I'll take you—as soon as the storm is over."

The storm was as short as it was fierce. In half an hour the rain slackened and the wind began to drop. In an hour the sun was shining.

"I think we can go now," Alex said, getting to his feet.

Alice laughed depreciatingly and took her heavy parka from a hanger in the kitchen.

"Gil will probably never let me live this down, but I'll feel a lot better when I know for sure that they're all right."

They went down to the lake shore and Alex filled his outboard motor with gasoline. He was just finishing when a canoe very similar to his approached.

"Fred Keash!" he exclaimed under his breath. What could bring him over from Government Island so soon after the storm? Fingers of fear stole icily about Alex's heart.

Alex ran out on the dock and squatted to catch the bow of his friend's canoe. Alice was half a step behind him.

"Did Gil get here?"

Alex jerked erect. Sweat moistened his palms, and his thin fingers fumbled with the beaded tie slide he was wearing.

The white man's wife spoke first.

"You mean he left Government Island before the storm?"

"*Ehe*." Keash glanced at her and then away quickly. "The wind came up so quick!" He gestured suddenly.

Alex looked out across the open water. If Gilbert and Billy had gone to one of the other islands there was a good chance that they had found a place of refuge. But from Government Island there was nothing except open water. A terrible chill took hold of him.

Alice was white and shaken. "Do—do you think you can find them, Alex?" she asked, her voice quavering.

"We'll go out and see." His gaze softened. "They probably got in some place and are waiting for the wind to go down before they come home."

180

"*Ehe,*" Fred put in quickly. "They'll probably come home before we get out to look for them."

Word that Gilbert and Billy Lathrop were missing spread quickly. The men on the island gathered, paired off and went roaring across the lake in the direction of Government Island.

"Want to come with me, Alex?" Fred asked.

"*Ehe.*"

"Can I go along?" Alice broke in.

They eyed her hesitantly. "Well—"

"If something's happened, I want to know it!" Her voice crescendoed dangerously.

"*Ehe,*" Alex agreed. "If you want to come along, you can."

She knelt in the bow of the long, narrow canoe and stared intently at the lake. Although it was only a couple of miles to Government Island there was a long sweep of water for the wind to whip, if it chanced to be blowing from a certain direction. And the storm of an hour before had come roaring down the slot as accurately as though fired from a rifle. Even one who had been born by the lake would have found the fury of the storm too much for his feeble skill. What chance did Gil have?

Alex tried not to think such things as they angled across the lake. Near Government Island Fred turned, went along the shore for several hundred yards and headed back. The other canoes were working the same area expertly. Using landmarks to guide them they covered the stretch of water between the two islands with great care.

Alice knelt in the bow of the canoe, her frail body stiff and unyielding and her hands clasped tightly to the gunwale on either side. At first she talked with her companions, making observations and questioning them. But then for an hour she said nothing. Alex also found conversation difficult, but for a different reason. If he talked with her how could he keep her from knowing the fear that was growing in his heart?

In midafternoon they went ashore briefly for more gas and

181

something to eat. Alex suggested that Alice stay in and rest, but she wouldn't hear of it.

"Don't you understand?" she demanded. "I *have* to go!"

They were halfway across the lake when another boat came racing in their direction. Both men were waving their arms wildly.

Alice was the first to see them.

"Look!" she cried. "They must've found something!"

Fred turned and sped toward the oncoming craft. In a few minutes they met. Both shut off their motors and drifted close together.

"We found something!" one of the men cried in Indian. His face was white and drawn and Alex could see that he was shaking violently. "Canoe! Turned over!" He gestured helplessly with his hand.

Alice gasped.

"Where?" Alex broke in. "Did you see Gil or Billy?"

The man shook his head, but there was no need for that. The answer was written in shock and horror on his face.

"*Kawin,*" he answered. "No, we didn't see either the man or the boy. Nothing except the canoe turned over."

He was speaking so rapidly that Alice could not catch what he was saying. But she didn't have to understand the words. She could read the shocked expressions on their dark faces. She did not move or cry out. The only sign that she understood lay in the fact that her hands tightened on the gunwales until her knuckles showed white, and new sweat glistened on her face.

"Ca-can we go over there, Alex?" she asked weakly, as though she was suddenly devoid of strength and reason enough to make her own decisions.

"Not now," he said gently. "I think we had better go in."

Somehow the people on the island seemed to know that they had discovered some form of bad news. As the canoe neared the dock, all the men and women on the island crowded down to the water's edge. Their blue and red and orange and green dresses and jackets sparkled brilliantly in the late afternoon sun.

Alex could hear Alice praying softly. He swallowed hard to keep back the tears. The canoe touched the dock and mechanically Alice got out. The women surged about her. Some were sobbing unashamedly. Tears trickled in silence down the cheeks of others.

Alex turned to his companion and started to speak, but checked himself. Fred too was crying.

* * *

The women of the village brought gifts of such as they had to Mrs. Lathrop. One woman cut up one of her dresses and made a skirt for her. A little girl brought a torn, faded bandana, carefully wrapped in a dirty piece of paper. Grandma Keash brought her most prized possession, a small travel alarm clock Gil and Alice had brought to her.

"I want you to have this," she said in Indian.

The white woman stared at it. She thought she understood what Grandma was saying, but couldn't be sure. She called Alex to interpret for her.

"Yes," he said, "she wants to give it to you. She says your son Billy was very dear to her because he would come over to her house and talk to her and try to learn her language. And she says she loved your husband as her own son."

Although they found the canoe the day of the accident it was the end of the week before they found the bodies. A commercial fisherman saw them washed up on the shore several miles away.

Alex was numb with grief. He could not eat. He could not think. It was unbelievable that his good friend was gone. And Billy! The boy who had been such a comfort to Grandma Keash only the night before his death. The boy whose faith was so strong, so positive, who was such an example to the people.

The day after the bodies were found the chief and two members of the tribal council called on Alice.

183

"We don't know where you plan to bury them," he said, "but your husband loved us and we loved him very much. We have a place in the center of our cemetery large enough for two graves. We would be honored to have them buried with our loved ones."

She began to cry.

21

Alex stood silently before the window in his living room, staring out at the bleak, gray skies. Clouds had moved in during the morning and a light mist was sifting down, just enough to fleck the glass with moisture and blot out the buildings on Government Island. It was cold outside and the hint of rain indicated it would get even colder before the wind whisked the clouds away to let the sun warm the forests and lake once more.

Alex's breath came in long, thin draughts. He saw, and yet he didn't see, so great was his agitation. His mind fumbled with the old familiar shapes of trees and dock and lake before him, confusing and blurring them. He knew they were there, but that was all. Time seemed motionless and the numb, aching dread that began cold in his stomach, engulfed his entire being.

The happenings of the past week were enough to confuse and bewilder anyone.

His friend was dead. Gilbert and Billy Lathrop had lost their lives in a useless little storm that scarcely lasted long enough to kick white caps on the lake. A storm so small and so sudden they probably didn't even know it was near until it swooped down upon them.

Why do things like this have to happen? he asked himself. *Why?*

Shivering, he turned back from the window. But only for a moment.

There was another question even more nagging, more persistent. Why had the Lathrops come north in the first place? That was the thing that tormented him.

Gil and his family didn't have to come to Island Lake. They didn't have to leave their fine home in the south with heat in every room and the water in little pipes. They didn't have to give up all the things that would make life easy for them, just to come to the Soulteaux with the gospel of Christ.

Alex thought about it often, especially during the week after the accident.

Gil only got support money from the mission, so it wasn't because he was well paid. And they didn't come because they had to. There could only be one reason. They had come north because they loved the Soulteaux and were concerned that they would have a chance to confess their sin and accept Christ as their Saviour so they could go to heaven.

Alex brushed his hand nervously across his forehead. He was both Christian and Soulteaux. The people Gil and his family came to reach were his own. And what was he doing to win them for the Lord?

Alex winced. Because his support money didn't come in when he thought it should, he was turning his back on them. Because he wanted an easier life for himself and his family he was no longer going to serve God.

He watched a woman, heavy with child, struggling up the

186

path. She was carrying a large pail of water in either hand. He scarcely saw her.

Death wasn't the only way a man could give his life for Christ, he reasoned. He could give it by living for Him. That was the way with Tom French, Phil Cramer, Craig Marshall, and Indian pastors and evangelists like Allan Harper.

His mouth pinched to a thin line and it was an effort even to breathe.

What about the Coopers? What if they had become discouraged and had left the work before he got to Round Lake. Where would he be now? Lying drunk in some trapper's cabin? In jail? Or would the witch doctor's prediction have come true? Would he be in an unbeliever's grave? What would have happened to him?

Whatever else would have been his lot, he wouldn't have known Christ as his Saviour. And that would have been the worst of all.

Suddenly his decision to go back to commercial fishing became all the more confused. God had called him to do a special work for Him. This was something he had never seen and understood before. What about the people he would have reached for Christ, if he stayed in full-time service? Would they go to hell? And if they did, would it be his fault?

The thought was staggering.

Slowly he turned back to his attractive young wife. "Rose," he said, his voice tight with emotion, "I'm going to write to the mission again. We'll stay."

Tears of joy stood in her eyes. "Oh, Alex." Suddenly she was in his arms.

❃   ❃   ❃

Several members of the mission board flew out to Island Lake for the funerals. Cramer took them back to the Pas after the service. The following week he returned for special meetings, asking Alex to help him.

"There's a good crowd tonight," the white missionary ob-

187

served quietly as the two of them stood at the back of the church.

"*Ehe.*" Since Gil and Billy's deaths there had been more interest in spiritual things at Island Lake than Alex could ever remember.

"Why don't you bring the message tonight?"

Alex nodded. He didn't know why, but he enjoyed getting up before the church and talking about Jesus.

"We only have a short life to serve the Lord," he said in his message. "We have to be ready to face Him when death comes."

The Indian pastor didn't mention Gil Lathrop in his sermon. He didn't have to. The missionary's grave and that of his son were in the center of the cemetery, speaking eloquently of the shortness of life and of the depth and strength of love. The people who crowded the church building were thinking about Lathrop and his family—and about the God they loved so much that they came north to tell the Indians who had never heard of Christ about Him.

Alex closed his message without giving an invitation. The people got up and filed out in silence. If anyone was stirred by what was said he kept it to himself.

The following evening Alex continued his talk where he left off.

"You all know about Joseph," he said, "how he resisted temptation when Potiphar's wife was after him. That's what God wants us to do. And not only with the temptation to be immoral. He wants us to resist the temptation to drink and gamble and all the other sins."

Isaac Kenette and Joe Keash squirmed miserably. They both had made decisions for Christ several years before. However, they had neglected their Bible reading and prayer and church attendance over the years, and were no longer walking in a way that would please God. All those things Alex knew.

Again he gave no invitation. But when the meeting was over they came hesitantly up to Alex.

188

"You speak about sin," Isaac said, shifting from one foot to the other.

"The Bible speaks about sin, Isaac," Alex reminded him. "I only tell you what God says in His Word."

There was another silence.

"God got through to me tonight," Isaac said at last.

Their gaze met.

"Did you listen?"

"Yeah. This time I listened."

Joe Keash spoke up. "It is the same with me, Alex." The slight, intense Indian pastor sat down with them.

"You want the sin out of your lives?" he asked.

"Yes." They both answered quickly—eagerly.

"You are ready to let God take over your lives?" Alex persisted. "You are ready to let Him lead you where He wants you to go?"

They both nodded emphatically. Alex read several portions of Scripture. At last he knelt with them in prayer.

There were others who made decisions for Christ during the remainder of the week. Several confessed their sin and accepted Christ as their Saviour. Others like Isaac and Joe came back to Christ.

This was something Alex had only tasted before. He had never really known the joy of leading souls to God.

"I thought it was wonderful to be a Christian before, Rose," he told his wife excitedly, "but I never knew how wonderful it could be until now." His smile faded. "And to think, I almost missed out on it. I almost turned my back on God and missed this joy."

❁   ❁   ❁

Phil Cramer came over to have supper with Alex and his family the evening before he was to go back to the Pas. Alex thought there was something strange about his manner, something he couldn't quite understand. Cramer talked about the meetings, the work of the Bible school, Alice Lathrop and the fact that she had decided to stay on with the mission.

189

"You know we are faced with the problem of finding someone to take over as principal now that Gil Lathrop is dead."

"Yes."

"The board has been giving a great deal of thought and prayer to it. We have to have someone who can get along with both the faculty and the students."

"Yes." It would not be easy to find someone to take Lathrop's place. He had a love for the students that few missionaries had. When problems arose that he had to deal with, the young men would listen to him well.

As for the faculty, Alex didn't know about that, but he figured Lathrop must have gotten along well with them too. After all, he was another white man. He ought to have been able to get along with his own kind.

"We've given a great deal of consideration to Lathrop's successor, Alex." He paused significantly. "And we're all agreed that we have come up with the right person for the job."

"Fine," he answered. "Who do you have in mind?"

Cramer nodded. And then a smile broke across his face.

"We want you to be our new principal, Alex."

He stared numbly at the guest. It wasn't true. It couldn't be. He was an Indian. Even the mission didn't put Indians in charge of white missionaries. And even if they did, they wouldn't have chosen him. He wasn't trained. He didn't have any education.

"You're joking!"

Cramer shook his head. "It's the truth, Alex. The only question any of us had was whether you would get discouraged and quit. When your letter came saying that you had decided not to leave the work the board asked me to put you in charge of these meetings and to spend enough time with you so I could decide whether you meant business when you withdrew your resignation. Last night I decided that you did." He paused significantly. "So the job is yours if you want it, Alex."

That night after the missionary returned to the place where he was staying Alex was still stunned.

"Think of it, Rose," he said, his voice rough with emotion. "We almost missed this—this blessing."

She smiled warmly. Tears were in her eyes.

"If I had let Satan keep me discouraged and take us out of the mission I wouldn't have this chance to serve our people."

She came over to him, looking up at him happily.

"That's true, Alex."

In the growing twilight he saw a young man walking up the path with a Bible under his arm. A young man who, for some reason, reminded him so very much of himself when he was a boy. This was the kind of young men he would be helping to train. And for what reason? So they could go out and reach their own for Christ.

"Yes," Alex said, joy ringing in his voice. "God is good!"